A FINE PLACE

A FINE PLACE

A NOVEL BY

Nicholas Montemarano

Context Books, New York, 2002

www.contextbooks.com

Designer: Johanna Roebas
Jacket design: Carol Devine Carson

Context Books
368 Broadway
Suite 314
New York, NY 10013

Library of Congress Cataloging-in-Publication Data

Montemarano, Nicholas, 1969–
    A fine place : a novel / Nicholas Montemarano.
      p.   cm.
    ISBN 1-893956-21-0 (alk. paper)
    1. Bensonhurst (New York, N.Y.)—Fiction.   2. African Americans—Crimes against—Fiction.   3. Italian American families—Fiction.   4. Grandparents—Fiction.   5. Ex-convicts—Fiction.   6. Hate crimes—Fiction.   7. Racism—Fiction.   I. Title.
    PS 3613.O57 F66 2002
    813'.6—dc21   2001005518

ISBN 1-893956-21-0

9 8 7 6 5 4 3 2 1

Manufactured in the United States of America

In memory of—
Mamie
Helen
Lucy Rose

CONTENTS

CONTENTS

A FINE PLACE

Chapter One

UNDER THE HIGHWAY

(August, 1989)

Someone held a bat. Someone said *listen* and the others found bats and they got into several cars. Some were angry and others made themselves angry. They drove to Nino's pizzeria and got out of their cars and waited. They stood on the corner and watched people come out with slices. The door opened and they leaned around the corner and looked. One of them looked through the window and said he did not see anyone inside, and someone told him to shut up and stand with the rest of them, and someone else said *let's just wait.*

Some held bats that had been designed and shaped and smoothed to hit a baseball; others held long flat pieces of wood. Someone slammed a bat against the ground, and the others heard this and did the same. They waited on the corner and listened for the door.

Someone said *there he is*, and someone else said *are you sure*, and one of the others said *shut the fuck up*, and someone slammed a bat or stick against the street. Someone said *nigger* and someone else repeated it, and those who were not yet angry made themselves angry.

One led and the others followed.

They ran and waved their sticks until they were tired and under a highway. Under the highway was a field of weeds and uncut grass. There was a tall wire fence and a dog sniffing along it, and there was nowhere to run when you reached the fence. It was difficult, with someone chasing you, to climb this fence and avoid the sharp wires on top and get over to the other side. It was more likely someone would grab your sneaker and pull you down. It was more likely you would let go, even if your hands held tightly the top of the fence. Your hands were likely to bleed and you would give up.

Someone swung a bat and someone else did the same. Some used the thin handle of the bat and others used the meaty part, which had been shaped to hit a baseball.

The dog ran through the grass and was gone.

Someone said *not so hard on his head, we don't want to kill him.* Someone dropped his bat and so used his fists; someone else used his feet. There was one who waved his arms and heard someone shout *nigger*, and he repeated this word and made himself angry.

Cars passed on the highway above: the rhythm of tires rolling over grids in the road; for a brief moment, through an open car window, music.

To someone on the highway above, it might have looked like the boys were dancing in the grass. To a child, it might have looked like these boys were trying to break open a piñada that had fallen to the ground.

It was easy to break someone using a bat; it was easy to make someone soft and broken that way, and it could start and end very quickly that way, and so someone dropped his bat and used his hands, and the others did the same and used their feet, and every bat was on the ground and the grass was wet.

Someone was tired and backed away to find his breath, and then he found it and moved to the front and used his feet. Others grew tired and someone said *let's go,* someone said *enough,* and those who were tired pretended they were not, and they reached into the grass and picked up their sticks or bats.

One ran, the others followed.

They got into their cars and drove to a school parking lot; they got out of their cars and waited. One of them said *what do we do with the bats,* and another said *what do you mean what do we do with them,* and someone else said *are you sure that was him.*

It was summer; the sun was setting. They sat on the hoods of their cars until the parking lot went dark, and then they got into their cars and drove home.

Chapter Two

WAITING FOR TONY

(December, 1995)

Tony was coming home, how could Sophia think of anything else—
her husband dead twenty years this day (she had not been to his
grave in five, but used to every year on this day), and her sheets
were wet this morning (these little things could be a sign of something serious, her sister Vera would say, you wake up with wet
sheets and three months later it's a bad kidney, and Sal would tell
her to shut up, you're nothing but a worry wart, it's no wonder
people stay away from you, and Sophia would feel sad about her
sister, how she would shut her mouth so quickly, but Sophia would
not say a word). So what if Sophia *did* think about other things—
that was the way her mind worked.

She got out of bed; she groaned; the sheets were wet.

And why so much fuss over Tony, who was not *her* grandson? He
had made his life for himself.

But the answer was there, an easy answer: he was a handsome young man, and he was Vera's grandson, and today could be a new start, today could be, again, young Tony at the head of the table (who knew if he still liked Sunday, five years could have changed him, who knew what he liked, but certainly he was still handsome).

Sophia smelled the sheets; the odor was not strong.

She was not his grandmother, she told herself. Sophia, you are *not* his grandmother! He belongs to Vera and Sal—let them have their day. Let Sal open the door for him; let him ask the questions. Let Vera light his cigarettes; let her change the channel. Sophia rubbed her eyes and imagined her sister hovering over Tony.

(In the apartment below, Vera fried eggs for Sal and thought: The barber said *beautiful* before my grandson's hair touched the floor.)

They had been waiting five years for Tony, and now it was today, but how would she pass the next five hours?

"Don't cook," Vera told her. "Not a single meatball. And don't forget, I know his favorites."

Well is that why he never visited his own grandmother, thought Sophia, even before he found trouble, is that why he showed up at *my* door looking for a meal, because *you* know what he likes?

Sophia would make meatballs; she needed to pass the time. Vera was known to not make enough: what if Tony reached for the gravy boat and found it empty? Why come home to that?

Sophia tried to picture Tony. It was almost impossible. But at night, when the stations were off and she finished her romance novel and she was up every half hour emptying her bladder, she saw Tony grinding his teeth, she heard wood smack against bone.

He was not capable of such violence, she thought watching her sheets soak in the tub (but that was years ago and he was *not* her grandson).

5

A boy was dead.

It was the others, he had said—his friends. Sophia never trusted them. They were wise guys, his friends; they had sharp tongues.

The boy's mother was in court every day and it was impossible to hate her. To the papers this woman said, *Justice*.

"Do you remember, we used to take him to the barber," Vera said to Sal.

"Watch the eggs—not too dry!"

"What curly hair he had!" (She hated to see his hair on the floor, such thick hair swept into a pile, but when she looked up his face was beautiful too, and she would tell him so, who cared if Sal yelled, who would spoil him if she didn't?)

"Your mouth is going and going and you don't watch what you're doing," said Sal. "And we never took him to the barber."

"Sure we did. The barber right next to the candy store."

"You're dreaming!"

"I'm sure about this," said Vera flitting around the kitchen with a spatula in her hand. "We would stop at the candy store and buy picture cards for him—"

"Watch the eggs!" (This is why no one comes around, Sal wanted to tell Vera. This is why our son shows his face every two years, and our grandson too before he got into trouble, this is why people run away from you, all this talk about the past, people don't want to hear that, who cares about baseball cards and how curly his hair was and what the barber said.) "And keep your mouth shut today," said Sal.

"What am I saying?"

"Don't treat him like a baby. He's a man—what is he, twenty-five by now?"

"What did I say?"

"He doesn't need you tying his shoelaces."

"He's our grandson. He hasn't been home in five years."

"You think he wants to come *here* today? You think he wants to hear about his hair?"

Vera turned off the stove.

"Why are you crying?" said Sal.

"The eggs are dry."

"Listen—he doesn't want to come here and see anyone crying."

"You don't like them dry."

"It's not the end of the world," said Sal. "So you'll make them again—it's five minutes out of your life!"

Vera scraped the eggs into the garbage.

———

Sophia wet her face, and at that moment—when she felt the arthritis in her hands, when downstairs Vera asked Sal to come over and look at his eggs so that they would be perfect this time, so that he would not have to wait another five minutes (he was reading the sports section and would not get up), when Sophia decided to go to the butcher for chop meat—she forgot Tony was coming home. It was a normal day.

It was a moment, and then she was dizzy again—today could be a new start! She felt a rush in her legs; she was young; her hands did not hurt. (But the sheets were soaking in the tub and her pacemaker was twelve years old; her dead husband's picture was on the wall.) No, she told herself, you will walk to the butcher like any other day, you will roll the meat into balls wearing an old housedress, and you

7

must sit in the back room when Tony arrives, you will not greet him at the door with a shaking lip, you will not—like Vera and Sal—make him feel like he never held a bat (in five years she had not been able to hate the dead boy's mother); you will *not* hold an ashtray under his cigarette.

Years ago, thought Sophia, just ten quick years ago, these rooms were filled. (Last week she sat at the kitchen table a whole day playing solitaire; the coffee table in the back room was covered with dust; the same butterscotch candy had been in the dish for months.) Years ago, there were people in every room on every floor. On Sunday, all three stoves were used at the same time.

But what did they have now?

They had two young men living on the first floor (where Sophia's mother, now in a rest home, had lived seventy years of her life. Imagine: the same walls for seventy years!).

And the neighborhood too was much different: so many businesses closing, restaurants losing money. And for what? Who gave the neighborhood its reputation? The newspapers, Sophia would answer if only someone would ask her. Bensonhurst is a good place to live, she would say. Never mind what you hear.

And Vera, her poor sister—she had not seen her son Gino in two years. It was better that way, Sophia told her sister, the way he picked on her, calling her a crazy woman. Who was he to say that to his own mother? He wanted to be a singer in Las Vegas! If anyone asked about Tony, Sophia would say: He's too much his father—he had the wrong friends and too many times someone told him he was wonderful. (Vera had a tissue ready before Tony sneezed.)

Now they were only three. Sunday nights they ate Chinese food.

It was Sunday. Sal changed his shirt. He lit a cigarette. (It's going to kill you, the doctor told him, but it's too late now, Sal told Vera, my lungs are black, and what about *my* lungs, Vera told Sal once, but she would not say that now; it was Sunday and he was going to see the butcher, his friend, and they would sit in the back of the store, as they did every week, drinking wine while the butcher's wife sliced meat). He laced his shoes.

"You're going out?" said Vera.

"What do you think?"

"Don't stay out all day."

Sal took his coat from the closet and walked to the door.

"He'll be here at two o'clock." Vera dropped a plate and the noise frightened her. She said she was sorry. (But it must be good luck, she thought—the plate did not break.)

"I don't want to come home and see you bouncing off the walls."

"What did I say?"

"You're a real dummy," Sal said. "Why would he want to come here?"

"I'm cooking. Where else would he go?"

"I'll come home at five o'clock and find you alone."

"Don't come home," Vera said. "You want I should tell him you had something better to do?"

"Wake up!" said Sal.

"Stop shouting."

"We're nothing to him!"

"What did I say?"

"He wants to find a girl," said Sal opening the door. "He wants to get laid."

Two o'clock, Vera thought—she could hear Sal walking down the stairs too fast (there was nothing she could do if his heart gave out;

9

she would not die from grief)—at two o'clock my grandson will kiss the top of my head.

———

Sophia dumped the candy into the trash and wiped the dish with a wet towel. She figured: how many more minutes until he comes, how many more things still to do? There was time, yes, but never enough. She started to wring out the sheets. But it was not so easy with stiff hands, and her knees against a cold floor.

As she squeezed the sheets she remembered a lazy Sunday, years ago, not so long before what happened with Tony—plump clouds drifting across the sky, her new potted plant on the fire escape. She watered the plant and sat in a chair. Tony's eggs made noise behind her. The potatoes were soft and waiting in a pan. She watched water fall from the leaves and into the soil, and she waited for the water to work through the soil and into the small plate which held the pot. The eggs were spitting, and she could hear Tony turning the news-paper behind her. She sat in the chair and watched water drop from the leaves and after much work gather in the plate.

What a safe morning that was—such quiet in the yard below and how easy the air came in through the open window.

Tony's eggs were begging to be turned (even now she remem-bered the sound), so she stood and did what they asked—a sprinkle of salt on each side—and there he was sitting at the table wetting his fingers to turn the page. She took a potato square from the warm pan and held it over his mouth. The potato was soft between her fingers and he did not look up from the paper, but he opened his mouth for her to drop the potato inside.

She sat in the chair—what a lazy breeze that day against her face.

Water ran over the side of the plate and fell on the plants in the garden below. She leaned out the window and looked down and saw where the water was falling. She watched the plate and waited for the next drop and followed it down. She did this a while with the clouds in new positions above her. What a lazy business that morning was. She watched a red bird perch on a wire; she watched it balance on the wire and walk along the wire and then she saw it fly away. She followed the clouds and saw that they were moving. Another drop from the plate, and then she poured more water.

She heard Tony shifting in his chair—how careless of her to forget his eggs! The butter was gone from the bottom of the pan. She turned the eggs and saw that everything was fine—not a single brown spot. She added salt to the potatoes. Did he want ketchup? Of course he wanted ketchup. She put the bottle on the table in front of him. She would let him add his own ketchup, and more salt if he wanted. Once she put on too much salt. How terrible to see him with an empty fork. But everything was fine (she remembered): she could not find a brown spot and the potatoes were soft and warm. She lay two pieces of toast on a plate and spread butter on the toast. She lay the eggs on top of the buttered toast and spooned some potato squares around the edge of the plate. The steam from the pan was sucked out the window. She stood behind him and watched him read the paper; he watched him wet his fingers to turn the page. He turned around and saw her standing there, and he moved the paper to the side and made room for the plate. She waited to hear him eat, and then she waited to see his head move closer to the plate and his fork moving up and down, and only then did she start to fry her own eggs.

Heat rose from the pan and wet her face. A breeze moved the leaves of the plant, and another drop of water fell into the soil. The water was working its way down. She stood over the pan and watched the plant on the fire escape; she watched the plate under the plant. The plate was filled with water, and she was waiting to see if another drop would fall into the garden. She was watching very closely, and then she felt Tony's hand on her shoulder. He was behind her, very close to her, and they stayed this way—eggs soaking up butter, clouds shifting.

After a while he asked if he could have a cup of coffee, and of course there was a fresh pot waiting.

But this was not a lazy morning with her knees against the floor and her hands stiff and so much to do before he came, and here she was daydreaming.

———

Vera did not want to think about it—Tony *would* walk through the door. Where else would he go? I walked him home from school, she thought (scrubbing the floor in the hallway where he once sat and shuffled picture cards), and waiting for him was a bowl of hot soup. The times they had here! Who could argue against that? They were good times.

But why did they stop?

First her son Gino stopped coming, then Tony (and it was *not* her mouth; she hated when Sal said that word: *mouth*: it made her less than anything). She did not want to think about it, but what went wrong? It was Gino first. Why did her son hate her so much? So bitter! She looked into his eyes and they were cold. It was Thanksgiving and he wanted to be anywhere else. He lived in California, he lived in Vegas, he was back in Brooklyn, he was a singer, he was buying a nightclub, he was doing impersonations (just to get my foot in the door, he told Sal, but Sal would never make fun of *him*). And what had it done to poor Tony, moving him around like a piece of luggage?

Imagine a grown man hanging out at clubs with a bunch of kids (she did not want to think badly of her son, but no one had heard from him in so long).

He was a DJ, he told Sal.

And what did Sal say? "Are you making good money?"

There was the week he thought he could make six figures selling vacuum cleaners—*her* Gino! Imagine trying to sell a vacuum to your mother.

———

It was cold enough for gloves. They were playing mambo music on the stoop next door and Sal wanted to run away from it. The dark girl waved; she was not wearing a coat. Her mother stood next to her shaking her hips. Sal nodded. A cop used to live there and now this! Years ago there were no cracks in the sidewalk; you didn't find dog shit on the bottoms of your shoes.

He finished his cigarette. He was out of breath; his lip was numb.

Watch this, he thought. Watch me do this.

He lit another cigarette and swallowed the smoke. (Until they close my eyes, he thought, and for a moment, laughing, he saw his body on a bed, and Vera would not know what to do with it.)

Why should he wait all day for a knock at the door? He would shake Tony's hand, offer him the best chair, and turn on the television. They would talk about the game. (He could hear Vera's crazy mouth: *Look at him—how handsome!*)

He walked two blocks and turned the corner at Eighteenth Avenue. He wanted to live at least ten more years.

To the three girls with their jackets unbuttoned; to the young man with a hearing aid; to all the people in the funeral procession passing him now—he wanted to say: *Watch me do this.* (He smoked his cigarette down to the filter.)

Someone shoved a flyer at him.

A boy on the corner was selling a cat.

<hr/>

Vera felt the deep scar on the top of her head, a chunk taken away from her. *Removal of a growth,* she would tell people (as she reminded herself when she looked into a mirror). *Benign,* she would add several seconds later (for suspense, she admitted). Her body was falling apart, it had been for years, but here she was well into her seventies, and she was going to wear a new sweater today.

She would get her hair done; she would brush her hair over the scar.

Vera let her nightgown fall to the floor. She sponged her face and neck, and then her chest and under her arms, where there was another scar (long and purple and old). She was sad about the scar, something more than the scar, she was sad about her old heart inside her chest, a few inches away from her hand when she lay her hand on her breast, but she was sad about something else—how long it had been since she sat in the tub for a warm bath! She was thinking about the stairs: how many steps until the bottom, how many steps until the beauty parlor: and after all that she would have to do it again. The first step down was the most difficult, but she could do it: with her new sweater and the pin Tony gave her one Christmas. The first step down was the only thing to do, it was one of the things your body did: it went down, it went up, it went to buy bread and chicken cutlets, it went to the doctor for tests, it went to church on Sunday, it went to the post office for stamps, it went to funerals and wakes, it sat on the stoop in warm weather, it watched people and walked to the corner and walked back and sat—the body went where it had to go. She should have taken the first floor apartment when her mother went into the rest home (Sophia told her to take it, she was always right). But how could she leave these rooms?

She squeezed the sponge; the water was cold.

There was the time she went out in a snowstorm for Tony, who sat on the floor and flipped baseball cards. Now that was a memory! (Vera stood in a trance now, thinking—but how could it be true?— that Tony was inside her head making her remember, and still he could make her walk to the store for one more card.) The rooms were filled with cousins and sisters and children, but Vera walked to the store with six inches on the ground. "Do you see how you spoil him?" said Sal. "Do you know what that does to a kid?" And when was *he* going to get up from his chair and stop the boy from crying?

Vera dropped the sponge into the sink. It was too early to get worked up, but Tony was only four hours away.

The last time Tony was here, she thought (pressing a towel against the place where her breast used to be), was the day of his trouble. It was a Sunday. She could think about that day for the rest of her life.

She was a great thinker.

She would do anything for a knock at the door.

———

Sophia put her hands under warm water. Her lips were cold.

(The tips of her fingers went numb in Vera's hands before they read the verdict; she squeezed; her sister squeezed back; they read the verdict.)

She had a backwards mind—it could not leave things alone. The boy's legs were broken, she read in the paper. His skull was fractured; his ribs cracked. He bled until his heart stopped. At the emergency room, doctors opened his chest and broke his breastbone to massage his heart. Everything she knew she knew from the papers.

The prosecutor said—"Tony Santangelo was the driver."

Vera said—"But he is such a good handsome boy!"

Sal said—"*They* are the racists!"

Gino said—"I know a good lawyer."

The defense said—"Tony Santangelo did not swing a bat."

The blacks had their version (there were speeches and marches and protests and vigils): *A boy drowned in his own blood. A boy was killed by the vilest form of racism we have ever seen. A mother no longer has her son. There is blood on the streets of Brooklyn. A boy is cold in the ground.*

Sophia remembered Tony's picture in the paper—walking down the courthouse steps in his gray suit, bodyguards on all four sides.

She rubbed her hands together and thought of the march—the Italians with their dirty mouths, the watermelons. She tried to wish them off the sidewalk and into their homes where they could say whatever they wanted; in front of the boy's mother it was an embarrassment.

At least they had watermelons, not bats.

Given the chance, thought Sophia stretching her stiff hands, the blacks would have ripped Tony apart in the street.

⎯⎯⎯

Vera placed a pill under her tongue; she breathed through her nose.

Ten seconds, she thought. Why is God giving me ten seconds with a pain in my chest? Why should *she* have a morning like this? She had had enough in her life: breast cancer; the growth removed from her head ("I think they took your brain by mistake," said Sal, and Vera laughed with him); now the heart condition that could kill her getting out of bed (she could end up lying on the floor for hours before anybody noticed). She breathed through her nose. The pill had dissolved.

Now which sweater would she wear for Tony—red or black?

⎯⎯⎯

"I would like to live another ten years," said Sal.

"Why not twenty?" said Carmine. "You're alive. You look okay."

Carmine's wife cut pieces of cold meat and lay them on the counter; she asked a customer to look at them; she was younger than her husband. And there she stood slicing meat while her husband talked away the afternoon and drank wine. She will stand there all day, thought Sal, and here is her husband sitting on a stool.

"I'm alive," said Sal.

17

"I'm alive too," said Carmine. His wife placed a cut of pork on the scale.

"Who said you weren't alive?"

"I'd like to live thirty more years. Ten is not enough."

"You won't live thirty years," said Sal. "That would make you one hundred five."

"You want me to die in ten years?"

"It makes no difference to me—live fifty more years."

"One hundred twenty!" said Carmine. "Now we're talking."

"Who wants to talk about death?"

"Who's talking about death? I'm talking *life*."

"It's a silly thing to think about," said Sal.

Vera needed to do *something*—chop vegetables for antipasto; clean the tub (in case Tony needed a shower); start the gravy (it was never too early). How many times in her life had she chopped tomatoes?

While the knife sliced cleanly through the tomato; while the juice spread on the wooden chopping board; while the smell rose to her face—she wondered what Tony was doing, and she wished (blood trickling from her finger: she was so careless lately) that he really could be in her head, that he could be inside her and make her know what he was doing (she saw him holding a tray; she saw him walking past open gates where a car was waiting—but that was the movies, she knew nothing about prison but through the movies; there was no tray; there was no car to take him home; she knew nothing).

She licked her finger but the blood did not stop; she rinsed the cut with cold water.

(And what was so important at the butcher shop? Not once in forty-five years had Sal lifted a finger.)

She was always giving, always doing things for Sal, for all of them, and what, she wanted to know, did she ever get in return? There was the time Sal and Tony were watching a football game and she tried to help, and what did she get that day but wisecracks? But no one had asked her to empty the ashtray: it was her pleasure; she did not care that there were only two filters. She dumped the ashes and crushed filters into the kitchen garbage pail; she wiped the inside of the ashtray with a wet paper towel; she wanted to make it back to them before they were ready for another cigarette. But she had an idea that day. She looked through the kitchen drawers; she looked in the bedroom closet and in the cabinets where she kept old dishes and silverware; she looked on Sal's desk and on the shelves above the desk; she looked behind his bowling trophies; she looked in her bottom drawer and in the closet where she kept extra blankets and her son's baby clothes; she looked in boxes she had not opened in twenty years.

How nice it would have been to find a second ashtray.

But what an idea she had!

She took the candy dish from the table. "Where are you going with that?" said Sal, and she thought: *Give me a minute. Please let me do this. How often do I have an idea like this?*

She took the candy from the candy dish and put it in a bowl she used normally for hot oatmeal cereal. For twenty years she had been using this bowl for soup and cereal and to crack and mix eggs, and why did it take her so long to have such an idea?

She wiped the empty candy dish with a wet paper towel. She waited for a commercial and went into the television room. "What happened to the butterscotch candy?" said Sal, and she placed the

19

bowl on the table in front of him. She placed the bowl in the middle of the table so that Sal could reach it and Tony could reach it. She saw that the ashtray was closer to Tony. She saw that Sal was reaching very far to tap his cigarette against the side of the ashtray. She stood there for a minute and saw that Sal sometimes tapped the ashes into his palm and then dropped them in the ashtray.

This was not good. This was not good for your back, and it was not good if you wanted to enjoy your cigarette.

She moved the ashtray closer to Tony. "What are you doing?" said Sal. "Do you think I have rubber arms?" And then she took the empty candy dish from behind her back and placed it on the table in front of Sal. "What the hell is this?" said Sal, and then he laughed and looked at Tony, and then Tony laughed and looked at her, and then she had no choice but to laugh with them. "What am I smoking—candy cigarettes?" said Sal.

"I had an idea," said Vera. "Why not two ashtrays?"

"Why not an ashtray and a candy dish?" said Sal. "That's what you thought."

"It's so you don't have to reach so far when you tap your cigarette," said Vera.

"She thinks we're smoking butterscotch cigarettes," said Sal to Tony (who stretched to see the television).

"It's not so bad," said Vera. "It looks like an ashtray."

"She says it looks like an ashtray," said Sal. "When was the last time you saw an ashtray without a place to hold your cigarette? Where on this candy dish do you see a place to put a cigarette?"

"It was a silly idea," said Vera reaching to take the candy dish back to the kitchen. She was not going to get upset. It would be very easy to move the candy from the bowl back to the dish. The bowl was much better suited for oatmeal. She was not going to cry here in front of her grandson: she could wait until she went into the kitchen. This was her new goal. She set this for herself as a goal—to control her emotions until she was out of their sight: in the kitchen moving the candy from bowl to dish, or later that night, after dinner, when she stood in front of the mirror and rubbed cream under her eyes (with the dishes waiting to be washed and Sal already in front of the television). It would be a pleasure to hold her emotions inside until she was out of sight. This was something she could do.

But Sal, as she reached for the candy dish, said, "Wait, it's okay. I like to hold my cigarette anyway. I like my fingers to smell like smoke."

And here she was, years later, still looking for something to do, still tying to please someone.

⸻

(Sophia waited at the back of the line.)

Carmine left Sal in the back of the store and went behind the counter to help his wife. Sal lit a cigarette and turned his chair away from the line. He listened to the customers:

"Can I have a different piece please? There's too much fat on this one."

"Excuse me, you went a little over on the cutlets. I asked for three pounds."

Why did Carmine not retire? thought Sal. Where was his family to take over the business? His two sons lived in California and his only grandson was retarded—that was why he did not retire! Yet he told Sal how much he loved the store: the smell of it; the feel of cold meat in his hands; the buzz of the slicer; the customers (listen to them argue over ten cents!). He wanted to live fifty more years for *this?*

Sal lit another cigarette. Half the line was gone. Carmine was back in his chair.

Sophia thought about leaving, but the line was shorter and the meat was for *her*, she remembered—today was like every other day, she could use the meat any time. And of course, even today, Sal was sitting at the back of the store with his friend. She knew why Sal was facing the wall—such a stubborn man! He would not say hello. Forty-five years he lived upstairs from her!

She left the line and walked over to Sal. "So today's the day," she said.

"Today is what?" he said, and stood with his hands in his pockets like a school boy.

(He knew she would say something about it; she was no different from her sister.)

"Your grandson," said Sophia.

"What about him?"

"What is this about Tony?" said Carmine.

"He's coming home!" said Sophia.

"He didn't say a word about it," said Carmine.

"This man," said Sophia, twisting her mouth at Sal, "could bury my sister at ten o'clock and be here by noon."

(And why not? thought Sal.)

Sophia ordered her meat.

But what shall I do when he knocks on the door? thought Vera.

I will let Sal get the door, she thought (but Sal was with the butcher, she remembered).

She stared into the pot. Bubbles rose to the surface of the water and Vera could not remember what she was doing; the bubbles popped and she turned off the stove; she tried to remember. Her finger was bleeding. Six plates were arranged on the table with a napkin and wine glass to the side of each.

(Gino had asked for Sal the last time he called, she remembered. How could she forget such humiliation? She answered the phone and Gino said, "Can I speak to my father, please?")

She wrapped a napkin around her finger. She removed one plate and one wine glass from the table. She brought them into the kitchen and put them away.

Bells were ringing.

She had forgotten about mass!

Stupid Vera! (and Sal would say it too). She had taken too much time with the pin on her red sweater and now bells were ringing. Too much time rearranging plates. The church was two blocks away. She imagined herself walking down the stairs. She counted the steps. She saw herself opening the front door and walking down the stoop (there was no railing and her legs were too short). How man' minutes for those two blocks? Not too many. (Did she have h￼ pills?) The stairs would take five long minutes, and outside s￼ would have trouble breathing in the cold air. If she could find son￼ one to walk with her. (Was she wearing the right glasses?) The￼ let was making noise. She should have taken the first ￼ apartment. Stupid Vera! The stairs were waiting for her. How ￼ times had she counted them? She checked her pill box—it wa￼

ter to be late for church than to die on the stairs. There were enough. Good. The lamp was on with a fresh bulb. The refrigerator hummed. Tony was coming in three hours and already she was short of breath. Her hand was on her breast, her old heart inches away from her hand.

"Your grandson is coming in less than three hours?" said Carmine.

"Who knows if he's coming?" said Sal.

"Who would know if not you?"

"He's either coming or he's not coming."

"What does that mean?"

"It means he might come and it means he might not come."

"But surely you know which one it is."

"If he comes, I'll know which one it is. If he doesn't come, I'll also know which one it is."

"Why would he not come?"

"What do I look like?"

"You just said he might not come."

"That's right."

"Who told you he might come today at two o'clock?"

"Gino called Sophia and told her that he talked to Tony and that Tony said he might be able to come today."

"Why did Gino call Sophia?"

"Who knows—ask Gino the next time you see him!"

"Where is *he*?"

"He might be in Vegas."

"Doing what?"

"Business."

"What kind of business?"

"Do I look like his secretary?"

"Is *he* coming today?"

"He might come and he might not come."

"Doesn't he want to see Tony?"

"Did I come here for twenty questions?"

"Can you take the garbage with your other hand?" said Vera to the young man who lived on the first floor. How nice of him to come up and help her.

One flight was nothing for a young man. But he would come back for the garbage (the stairway was much too narrow). "Do you remember when I asked you about the music?" she said to him. "Do you remember when the music was too loud and I asked you to turn it down?" (He had a tight grip on her arm; his legs were so much longer than hers.) "I asked you to turn down the music," she said, "and for a while, for a few weeks, you did not listen to me." (She would renew her pills next week.) "I tried to sleep," she said. "I tried to watch television, but your music was too much. And I remembered that I had asked you to turn it down, and I was mad at you. I'm not afraid to tell you because you are a nice young man, but I was mad at you." (Each step was a leap; she imagined what it would be like to walk down the stairs in silence.) "I thought about knocking on your door, but I said to myself, wait Vera, you asked him and he's a nice boy." (His fingers pressed into her arm. She wanted him to say something.) "And sure enough," she said, "you turned off the music. And I said to myself, Vera, do you see what I told you, he's a smart boy. But the funny part," she said (her heart struggling

25

inches away from his hand), "was that I could not fall asleep. I was up and down all night. It was too quiet. Isn't that something?" she said, walking down another step.

"Just a few more," he said.

There: he said something. (Should she give him a dollar?)

He helped her down the stoop. At the bottom she squeezed his hand. "That was a funny story I told you," she said.

He smiled and told her to stay warm.

She opened her purse. She looked up and saw him turning the corner. She put the dollar back into her purse. (And what about the garbage?)

In a few hours he could pass me on the street, thought Sophia—but why would he stop?

She turned from the wind and blew on her red hands.

She hit him in the face once, she remembered. What a devil he was that day, but she could not remember what he was doing. She chased him all over the apartment, and every time he ran out of her reach she was thankful that she had not been able to have children. But that was not true—she had wanted a child. Who did not want a child? Who did not want a handsome son? Yes, she had wanted one, and her husband wanted one too, but they would never have a son and it was her fault, and what did they do with their lives except take care of other people's children? But Tony made them most proud; they showed him off as if his curly hair came from them. And what was so special? He was a boy. He was not theirs. But now she remembered (fitting the key into the front door)—he was scratching her walls; he had taken a knife from the kitchen drawer and was using it to scrape the paint off her bedroom walls—that was why she hit him. How he cried and cried, and Sophia spent the rest of the night taking it back.

Tony could not take it back—that night.

There was a bat and Tony was there and a boy's skull had been cracked. And did it really matter who held the bat? If you were there and you were yelling *nigger*, was your hand not on the bat? No, she did not believe that—it *did* matter who swung the bat and Tony was not the type. He had been there that night and maybe he said a few bad words (he had always been a follower, she thought), and sometimes Sophia could see him holding a bat and she could hear the boy's ribs breaking; she could see a crowd of young men, all of them holding bats and pipes and sticks; and she could see Tony's sweaty face above the half-dead boy. She could see his fingers digging into the wood; but when she tried to imagine him bringing the bat down on the boy's face it gave her a chill and she gave it up. She could go so far and something made her give it up.

But it *had* to matter—who was able to swing the bat and who was not.

Tony was not capable, Sophia told herself—why else would she get such a chill?

———

Always pray for someone else, Vera told herself (passing the collection basket, making sure she was seen dropping in a dollar), but she could not help it: she prayed for her old heart. She sat in the last row and when it was time to kneel she remained in her seat. Her feet did not reach the floor. She prayed for Tony next: that he would arrive safely and that he would stay out of trouble. Next for her husband: that he would learn to show compassion. Then for the young man who helped her down the stairs: that the next time he would remember the garbage. (She should have given him a dollar.) Finally she prayed for the boys who went to prison, and for the one who was killed, and for his mother.

"Are you going home at two o'clock?" said Carmine.

"I don't know," said Sal, and then they were quiet.

The quiet made no difference to him—after all, he came here to smoke, not talk; this silence was beautiful compared to the chatter at home. Here he had smoke in his face, and his mouth tasted like smoke, and his fingers and shirtsleeves smelled like smoke, and he *would* live another ten years.

He laughed. Carmine poured another glass of wine.

It will knock out Vera's wind, thought Sal. Her legs will buckle. It will kill her if Tony does not come.

"When was the last time you spoke to Tony?" said Carmine.

"I don't remember," said Sal.

"Maybe today."

"Maybe." Sal looked at his watch and saw that it was past noon.

"I'm not close with my grandson," said Carmine.

"Tony treated me like a brother," said Sal.

"I don't get along with my brother."

"He asked me to go to the bars with him and his friends, and not once did I take a dollar out of my pocket."

"That's respect."

"His girlfriends kissed me if he told them to."

"On the lips?"

"On the cheek, on the lips, wherever."

"You were one of the boys."

"I was out once a month with my grandson."

"I can see why," said Carmine, and Sal imagined Tony walking into the apartment later that afternoon. They could sit opposite one another and share an ashtray. It was Sunday—they could watch the Giants. What would Tony do in the apartment with those two women? They would feed him—that's what they did, that was their life: it was all about the mouth: moving the mouth, eating when there was nothing to say, talking nonsense when their bellies were full. He had to be home by two o'clock—if only for his grandson's sake. Tony did not want idle chatter. He wanted a smoke on the stoop, a quiet moment outside with cold air on his face and his grandfather standing next to him. They would not need to say a word: standing on the stoop with the sun going down, the women inside, smoke on their fingers—that was enough.

Who knew his grandson better than he did? They had spent time together—quiet time, not chatter time; they had memories that had nothing to do with eating or talking; they had their ways together, their routines: for example, he always lit Tony's cigarette before his own.

He remembered one Sunday years ago: he and Tony stood on the stoop and watched a young man sweep leaves from the sidewalk in front of the building next door.

And how wonderful it was to see Tony inhale smoke, for Sal was seeing his own future—what he was about to do in a few seconds—

and already he could taste the smoke and he could smell it on his fingers and later he would smell it in his hair and his wife would complain about it and when he went to bed he would smell it on his shirt and if he could not sleep he would lift the shirt to his nose and think of the man next door, much younger than he, sweeping leaves into a neat pile by the curb, and how funny to see his future in his grandson, and now, finally, he breathed in the smoke and watched it come out of his nose and watched it disappear in the air above him.

What a quiet afternoon that was, with his wife at the beauty parlor and the football game to start in ten minutes. They had a six-pack of beer; they had a full candy dish and three types of nuts.

But what he remembered now, years later, sitting in the butcher shop, was Tony coughing. He remembered that Tony could not stop and that he dropped his cigarette on the stoop and held his chest. He remembered Tony choking and the man making sure a single leaf did not blow away. Sal did not ask if his grandson was okay. He did not say: *Can I do something for you? Can I get you a glass of water?* He smoked the rest of his cigarette and saw that Tony's eyes were wet and he was bent over trying to breathe. At one point, his cigarette almost gone, he put his hand on Tony's shoulder. But it was very quiet—leaves pushed to the curb and then pushed into a garbage pail on its side. He waited for Tony to find his breath, and not for one moment did he worry. It was a breezy day with brown and red leaves on the ground and some waiting to fall from the trees. The football game was important. For a week he had been reading about this game in the papers. He heard people talking about this game on the radio, and he called Tony and asked him to come over. "I'll send your grandmother to the beauty parlor," he said, and Tony, without Sal having to ask, brought a six-pack of beer, and for no one else would he bring anything. People were betting on this game, and it would be three hours sitting on a couch next to Tony, and they had plenty of nuts and he had almost a full package of cigarettes. But Tony, before the game, was coughing on the stoop, and how could that young man have spent such a day sweeping leaves? What would have happened to the leaves if he had not touched them? They would have gone somewhere else. Not once in his life did he pick up a leaf, and he was a happier man for it. He kept his hand on Tony's shoulder, and still he was bent over with a red face, and he saw that his grandson was about to spit on the stoop. That was fine. Everything went away and took care of itself. Eventually it would rain and the spit would go away and become something else. *Go ahead,* thought Sal, and Tony made a noise in his throat; he spit and shook his head. Tony was taking deep breaths, his face less red, and already Sal was lighting another cigarette. The game was starting in a few minutes and still this young man next door was filling so many bags with leaves. Sal handed the cigarette to Tony. A breeze blew the smoke and he could smell it around his face and he could taste it on his lips.

But what really made him happy that day was this:

The Giants scored a touchdown in the last minute of the game. It was a pass play, and the ball was deflected by two players before it was caught in the end zone. There was a moment when both he and Tony thought that the ball would not be caught, or that it would be intercepted by the other team. This moment was not very long, a matter of seconds, but he and Tony stood up and moved closer to the television set and when the receiver cradled the ball in the end zone and the referee raised his arms to signal a touchdown, Tony said,

"Holy shit, did you see that?" and Sal said, "What a play! Did you see that play?" and it became something they could talk about. For example, later today, Sal might say to Tony, "Do you remember that touchdown at the end of the Giants game five years ago?" and Tony might say, "That was something."

Tony ran out of cigarettes. "Here," said Sal as Tony was leaving. "Take these. Here. Take a few just in case."

Sal stood on the stoop and watched Tony walk to his car. He saw Tony light a cigarette; he watched smoke rise from Tony's mouth and then he looked into his pack and saw that there was one left for himself. He walked to the corner store. On his way back to his apartment, he smoked a cigarette and he knew that Tony was somewhere else driving through Brooklyn and that he also was smoking and he knew that he had been the one to give the cigarette to Tony, and this was his grandson who came over to watch the game when maybe there was something else to do.

But what made him happy, really, was that the sidewalk in front of the building next door was already covered with leaves.

What didn't make him happy now was that years had passed since the last time he and Tony watched a football game together, or smoked on the stoop.

But he would *not* go home at two o'clock—that was much too early.

Did they think he was waiting to run home? Five years had passed and nothing had changed: it was Sunday and here he was sitting with the butcher. He was older; he was shorter. He had survived five years without his grandson. He could wait until three o'clock.

"It's almost twelve-thirty," Carmine said.

"I have a watch," said Sal.

Ice shifted under Vera's soft black shoes. She took baby steps. People walked on the ice and held one another. Vera reached.

First pray for others.

But when was the last time she enjoyed a warm bath?

People held each other. She held her keys tightly in her hand. She reached and almost lost her balance. She thought of herself last—but why did *she* not deserve attention? She stopped walking. Ice was spread out in front of her. Legs came at her and walked on the ice next to her and came very close to her. It would be much easier to sit on the ground; it would be easier to let others take care of her. People walked at her and past her and into church for the next mass.

She prayed for the people whose legs came at her.

She started to move her feet. Her lips were dry and she tried to wet them with her cold tongue. She would not make it to the beauty parlor; she would not brush her hair over the scar on her head.

There was too much ice under her shoes. Why would God give her five minutes like this?

She prayed for the people who were late for mass. She prayed for Tony, such a handsome boy. Her lips were cold. She stopped and waited for the others to come at her and past her. (It would be much easier if she fell to the ground.) People walked against her and brushed past her and held each other. She dropped her keys. She reached for them and she was close to the ground and she reached down where the people walked. The ice stretched in front of her and she was low to the ground. Her keys were too far away; the ice came up at her and touched her.

She waited on the ground and asked for nothing.

"This girl took off her clothes," said Sal. "This was in the city. We were in a hotel room, and Tony was there and I was there and all his friends who bought me drinks were there. And this girl," said Sal pouring himself another glass of wine, "was taking off her clothes in front of me and Tony in the same room."

"Like brothers," said Carmine.

"It was a bachelor party for one of his friends. We had a nice dinner, we had some drinks, and then we were in a hotel room with a naked girl. She took off her clothes in front of us. She did a dance in the middle of the room with all of us in a circle around her and the guy getting married on the bed with his shirt off."

"You were having a great time."

"And when she finished dancing, she took off his pants."

"The guy getting married in the bed?"

"Sure. She pulled them down and he was busting out of his briefs. He was out to here," said Sal holding his arm out in front of his body, "and we all laughed and yelled at the girl to pull down the rest."

"She's getting paid. Why would she not do it?"

"So she pulled the rest down, and then she rubbed oil on his chest and on his legs and then she went for his prick."

"And you and Tony were watching together."

"I was watching with my grandson. We were standing right next to each other while she was pulling at this guy's prick and rubbing it with oil and dancing on the bed."

"You were getting a real show."

"The poor guy went limp with all the excitement. There were too many people watching."

"Who could blame him?"

"Tony slipped her a few extra bucks, and then she came up to me and rubbed herself on me."

"Your grandson did this for you. He thought that much of you."

"He asked me to go with him," said Sal. "He begged me for weeks."

<hr>

Vera reached for her pill box; she looked up at a naked branch. A man stood above her and asked if she was hurt. I need a pill, she wanted to say (as the man reached for her arm), but the ice was hard and she had fallen on her side; she needed this man's hand on her arm more than she needed a pill (but Tony was coming). Legs came at her and stopped near her face and people held each other above the ice and asked where she hurt.

People turned her onto her back.

The world had been turned: ice pressed against her back; she was falling into the sky.

A man placed a pill under her tongue.

It is better to die in bed than on the street, she thought. Or was one place better than any other?

They laid her on a stretcher and picked her up and carried her over the ice and into the street. They carried her closer to the flashing lights and slid her into the back of the ambulance. (Did someone have her keys?) The door slammed near her feet and a man pressed his finger against her neck.

<hr>

Sophia sat on the edge of a tub and waited for the water to drain.

Tony is not coming here, she thought, and he is not my grandson.

35

The drain gurgled; the last of the water was sucked down. It was after one o'clock. The wet sheets were heavy on the bottom of the tub. Her knees were pressed against the floor; a chill spread from her legs to her back. She squeezed the sheets; more water dripped into the tub and was sucked down the drain.

She climbed into her sheetless bed, a warm towel wrapped around her hands. She would visit her husband's grave, she decided. He died in this bed, Sophia thought looking first into the empty sitting room (with an empty but clean candy dish) and then into the kitchen (she had left the meat on the counter).

Years ago there were people in these rooms, thought Sophia—but that was life: you could not say it was good nor could you say it was bad. And now, with her eyes closed and a freezing rain tapping against the window, Sophia thought again of Tony's picture in the paper: he looked angry; she could not say that he did not look angry—staring at the protesters with his chin raised, a trench coat through his arm; she imagined him walking slowly to the cab; he hated the black people and their signs; he hated the boy for dying, hated him so much that given the chance he would crack his skull again, he would raise the bat above his head and—

She felt a chill and opened her eyes.

⸻

This is what the end will be like, thought Vera as the men wheeled her through the doors and into the emergency room. Young doctors stood next to her; people watched; hands touched her and she felt safe.

I would like a doctor to fix me, thought Vera—from the scar on my head to my short legs.

"I took all his baseball cards and put them in order by year," said Sal. "Those cards are worth thousands of dollars and I bought every one."

"He'll never forget something like that," said Carmine.

"My doctor said I should watch out for the mole on my ankle," said Vera.

"So you had a little fall today?" said the doctor pressing his hand gently against her hip.

"I told him to remove it," said Vera, "but he didn't want to do it." (Sal teased her about that too—nothing was safe. *I'll take it off for you,* he said holding a butter knife.)

"Do you have any pain in your side?"

"I have a scar under my arm and another on my head," said Vera.

"Did you feel any pain when you fell today?"

"I was on my side," said Vera. "I fell on my side and people were walking past me and I didn't know if anyone would stop to help me." (*You're always looking for attention. Everything is a show!*)

The doctor touched her hip and watched her face.

"It was terrible," said Vera. "I had to put a pill under my tongue." (*When will they invent a pill to make you shut up?*)

The doctor wrote something on the chart and asked Vera how she was feeling now.

"I'm a little excited. Does someone have my keys?" (The gravy was not made; she had forgotten to empty the ashtrays. Had she remembered to buy a card for Tony?)

"I don't think we need to keep you here very long," said the doctor.
"But it hurts," said Vera closing her eyes.

———

Sal smoked a cigarette in a chair in the back of the store. It was after
three o'clock. Carmine was getting ready to close the shop. He
cleaned the slicer and his wife wiped the counter. (A quiet moment
on the stoop, thought Sal, and our fingers will smell like smoke.)

———

Faces leaned over Vera and came down closer to her and asked how
she was feeling. She needed a cup of water and someone brought it
right away.

———

"Say hello to your grandson," said Carmine.
Sal stood at the door and looked at his friend and did not know
what to say. He waved and stepped outside. Carmine locked the
door. The cold began to work its way into his fingers. It was raining
and the streets were quiet. There were only so many blocks to walk,
and then what?

———

Sophia held a damp towel and listened to the freezing rain hit the
window. She sat up in bed and closed her eyes and the rain was all
she knew.

"Sorry I missed the party," said Sal after he closed the door behind him.

"Why did you come home if you didn't think he would be here?" said Sophia from the kitchen, where she prepared the salad.

"The football game is on." Sal turned on the television and took off his shoes. He dried his head with a towel.

"You're a selfish man," said Sophia. "You don't even ask where your wife is."

"Do you want me to ask?"

"Go ask yourself a question."

"I'm asking you," said Sal. "Do you want me to ask where my wife is?"

"Ask whatever you want," said Sophia.

"Everyone likes to play games."

"I don't know where she is," said Sophia. "Maybe you should worry for once."

"What can I do? Do you want I should start a manhunt? Maybe she's out on the street looking for Tony."

"You're a tough cookie," said Sophia. "You've got it all under control."

"He comes if he comes." Sal turned up the volume on the television.

"Remember you said that," said Sophia.

"I knew he wouldn't come."

"Who are you fooling?" said Sophia. "You thought he would be here."

"I'm watching the game. Do you see *me* making a salad?"

Sal fell asleep. Sophia played solitaire; she checked the meat between games.

If only she could make time pass more quickly. Her fingers ached with every flip of every card. Sal snored in his chair and she envied him for it.

She turned off the stove and thought she heard something. She stood in the kitchen and tried to breathe very quietly, and then it came again—yes, a knock at the door. She came out of the kitchen and listened.

"Did you hear that?" said Sophia.

"What?" said Sal coming out of sleep. "What's the problem now?"

"Someone is at the door."

"I suppose it's Tony," said Sal.

"Why would it not be him?"

"You never learn."

"Who could it be?" said Sophia.

"Just open the door," said Sal. "For Christ's sake—it's probably your sister. Maybe she remembered how to get home."

Sophia opened the door slowly, not without hope, and there stood Vera, short of breath, her hand against her chest. "If I tell you what happened to me," she managed to say. "Oh Sophie, what I went through. Here, take my bag, please, wait until I tell you."

"What happened?" said Sophia taking Vera's purse.

"What happened now?" said Sal who had not moved from the chair in front of the television.

"I was in the hospital," said Vera. "I thought it was over . . . oh

40

my Lord . . . if you could have seen me on the ground. Sophie . . . Take me to bed . . . please . . . I was on the ice, on my side . . . One minute I was standing outside church, and the next minute . . . oh God," said Vera crying (and cursing her short legs as she got into bed). "I thought it was all over."

"What happened?" said Sophia.

"She just told you what happened," said Sal walking into the bedroom. "She fell on the ice and got another scar on her head."

"Scar—what?" said Vera. "I'll give you a scar on your nose."

"Every day is a crisis," said Sal.

"I never made the gravy," said Vera. "What will he eat when he comes."

"What happened at the hospital?" said Sophia.

"I had a nice young doctor. He told me I was very lucky. He said, 'Vera, you're lucky you didn't break your hip.' "

"Did he take pictures?" said Sophia.

"What pictures?" said Vera. "Who took pictures?"

"Did he look at pictures of your hip?"

"I didn't see any pictures." (She had forgotten to make ice cubes, but she was sad about something else.)

"Always have them take pictures," said Sophia. "You never know what might show up."

"If you had a hang nail," said Sal, "you would have them take an X-ray."

"Listen to him," said Sophia. "He smokes those cigarettes all day and he wants to talk about health."

"He's killing me with the second-hand smoke," said Vera. "That's what the doctor told me."

"He doesn't listen," said Sophia.

41

"I'll never quit." Sal exhaled smoke for Vera to breathe.

"My lungs are bad," said Vera.

"He doesn't care," said Sophia. "Look at the look on his face."

"My pills," said Vera. "They're in my pill box in my purse."

"I've never taken a pill in my life," said Sal.

"Who are you fooling?" said Sophia.

"I can live to be a hundred if I want," said Sal.

"I need a pill under my tongue," said Vera, who would from this moment pray for others first.

Her mouth tingled; the pill dissolved. "Help me up," she said. "Bring me to the kitchen."

Sophia lifted her sister from the bed and walked her out of the bedroom and past the chair where Sal was sitting. "So you're still alive," said Sal, but when he saw Vera stare at the floor, when he saw that she would not look up, he said that he was only joking. "You know how I am," he said. "Since when can you not take a joke?"

"You've always had a fresh mouth," said Sophia (who was thinking of the salad: that she needed to finish it).

"Who has a fresh mouth?" said Sal. "I was only making a joke."

"You make too many jokes."

"I said I was sorry."

"You never said you were sorry."

"Who are you—her lawyer?"

"What's the score of the game?" said Vera.

"Stand there and wait until they put it on the screen," said Sal.

"Do you see the way you talk to her?" said Sophia.

"Jesus Christmas," said Sal. "That's just the way I talk."

"Don't stand there and listen to him," said Sophia.

"I'm trying to watch the game," said Sal.

"All of a sudden I can't stand here?" said Vera.

"Why would you *want* to stand there?" said Sophia.

"Who's making you stand there?" said Sal to Vera.

"I'm waiting for the score."

"Since when do you care about the score?" said Sophia.

"Who's making her stand here?" said Sal to Sophia.

"I can't stand where I want in my own apartment?"

"I don't know why Tony would want to come here," said Sophia.

"That's the smartest thing you've ever said," said Sal.

"I'm talking about *you*. Why would he come here to hear your big mouth?"

"I'm the only reason he would come here!" Sal stood up from his chair and turned down the volume on the television. "You think he would come here for chicken cutlets? You think he would come to see *you*?"

"I don't think he should come. When did I say he should come here?"

"You're *nothing* to him."

"But he would come for you?"

"You don't know anything about my grandson," said Sal moving closer to Sophia, his finger pointed.

"Who knows anything about Tony?" said Sophia. "You think you know something?"

"I want you to ask him when he gets here. Ask him who he comes here to see."

"So now you think he's coming?" (Sophia felt a rush in her legs.)

"Of course he's coming," said Vera.

"This place means nothing to him," said Sal.

"Listen to how he talks about his grandson," said Vera.

"Let's hear your answers," said Sophia, pointing back at him. "Tell us what you know about your grandson."

"Let me finish the salad," said Vera.

"You can't stay still," said Sal to Vera. "If someone offered you a million dollars to stay still and shut up for a full minute, you couldn't do it."

"Look who can't shut up," said Sophia.

"Today is no different from yesterday," said Sal. "All this fuss for what?"

"I want to know what you know about Tony," said Sophia.

"If I want to chop a green pepper, I can chop a green pepper," said Vera.

Sal sat in his chair and turned up the volume on the television. He wanted Vera to move away from him and into the other room where she could look out the window and count raindrops.

"You don't know anything," said Sophia.

"Maybe one day *I* won't come home."

"Don't talk like that," said Vera who was going to cry if she did not walk into the back room and lie down for a moment.

"Why do you think we never see our son?" said Sal. "He's smart for running away."

"Run away—what?"

"Don't listen to him," said Sophia.

"Everyone runs away." Sal looked at the veins in his hand. He wanted to live ten more years.

"But there were good times," said Vera picking at the cut on her finger.

"A meatball for lunch?" said Sal (who had been shoulder to

shoulder with Tony in the hotel room). "You think a meatball makes a good time?"

"Don't listen to him!" said Sophia.

Vera went into the back room and pressed her face against the window. Sal muted the television and closed his eyes. Sophia ran warm water over her stiff fingers.

There was nothing now but the rain against the window.

Chapter Three

SUNDAY

(August, 1989)

He stood on the corner, close to the wise guys he knew but did not know, and he wanted more than anything to disappear. He had sliced his last slice of meat; the rest of the afternoon and more importantly the night lay ahead of him. He was smoking a cigarette, the first from the package, and that was one more reason to be happy. But certainly he had *not* sliced his last slice of meat, he thought, and erased with this thought was his happiness, or at least that part of it linked to his future. But still there was today, the rest of it, and tonight, all of it, and still, most importantly, there was the cigarette between his lips, and there were nineteen more just like it, there were millions more, always more, and *that* was something he could count on.

He could not count on the wise guys on the corner (he knew

them but he did not know them). They were dressed for summer: shorts that went below their knees, white deck shoes, no socks, white tank tops, gold chains around their necks. There were four or five of them standing on the corner, one leaning against a pole, one against a fire hydrant, one brushing back his hair, one with his chest pushed out, all of them peering into each car that passed along the avenue. Copies of each other—same hair, same clothes. And what were they looking for? They were looking for girls, of course—girls other than the ones they called their girlfriends. They were looking for *paisans* who could offer them a smoke, or who they could give a smoke. They were looking, mostly, for someone to look back at them—some poor sucker rolling by in his car, someone lost per-haps, someone who did not know that a person's head could be cracked open for looking back.

It was late afternoon. The day had been hot, and most windows above the row of shops were open. Tony smoked his cigarette and looked into the windows: an old man adjusting a television antenna; his wife holding a piece of foil to wrap around it; a young woman pressing a towel against her forehead. There was a woman picking oranges from one of the many crates placed in front of the fruit and vegetable store. A younger woman, perhaps the daughter, was feel-ing the cucumbers. One of the wise guys pointed to her and another made loud kissing sounds; another asked her how the cucumbers felt today, were they big enough for her. They moved closer, but the old woman removed a house slipper and threw it at them. They scattered and laughed at her—what a great pitching arm she had, wasn't she one of the old Brooklyn Dodgers, and so on—and finally, when she went to retrieve her slipper, they gave her a round of applause (to impress the daughter, Tony knew). The young woman smiled at the boys, and Tony looked away, thinking that the city, every normal person in it, had gone crazy from the heat. The daughter was pretty in an old-fashioned way (she too was wearing a house dress and her dark hair was pinned away from her face), and for a fraction of a second, while the wise guys were making their play, Tony had imagined himself with her, had imagined himself carrying her bags (and her mother's bags) up to their apartment, imagined kissing her, or perhaps not even kissing but simply *telling* her that he wanted to kiss her (as in: he was a gentleman, he was not a wise guy, there would be other days)—all that in a fraction of a second.

And then it was gone—he would never know her. And then *she* was gone, and one of the wise guys had followed her into the store, and next week, Tony thought, he would not be surprised to see them together.

But he could count on his friends—he had spent almost every night this summer with them, and always they did the same things: they drank beer in the park, broke empty bottles against trees, poked fun at one another, cursed their jobs, their families, the world, the rotten beer they were drinking; they hated each other, fought with each other, cursed the neighborhood, the same old stinking neighborhood, cursed the wise guys, the *paisans* on the corner who got all the girls; they cursed anyone who had a good job, anyone who ever went to college; they drank more beer and made each other laugh, and eventually, reluctantly, they agreed that their families were not so bad after all, the world was not such a terrible place, and the neighborhood—well, it was the neighborhood, the only one they would ever have (unless they went to college and got a good job and bought a nice house on Long Island); the beer was not so bad, they agreed; they loved each other after all; a job was a job; the world was the world.

And each morning—the beer from the previous night a burden more than anything else—Tony cursed his friends and thought, with certainty, that without them he would be much happier. But without them, he also thought, he would be nothing.

He wanted to disappear now (he finished his cigarette, stepped on it). So that he could walk into his grandparents' apartment (where he and his father had been staying the past few weeks); so that he could take a long shower, wash from his body the smell of salami and ham; so that he could sit alone, unseen, and watch the Mets on television; so that he could leave the apartment without saying a single hello, without asking any of the cousins about college, without eating a single meatball or having a conversation with his great-grandmother, who was very old and very sick and could speak only a few words in English.

He could not count on privacy—he had none.

He could not count on his father to stay in the city longer than a few months.

He could not count on himself, Tony Santangelo, to be polite to his family. (But your family is your family, he told himself.)

He could count on his friends: that they would be in the park tonight; that they would be there every night.

$$\equiv$$

He walked down the street, past the row houses he had passed many times; he walked slowly, making sure as he moved closer that no one was standing in front of the building in which he now lived.

They would be on the third floor by now, he thought—all of them, cousins and nephews and crying babies, all waiting for the next plate of food to be carried out from Sophia's kitchen.

He looked up at the window and saw that no one was sitting there; he went inside.

The stairs rose in front of him.

If he could walk quietly up the old stairs; if he could slip into his grandparents' apartment and wash from his body the smell of meat; if he could dry himself and get dressed before one of them could come down from the third floor (certainly someone would hear the water running and fear a burglar); if he could do all of this, unseen, unheard, then the day, the rest of it, and the night, all of it, would be his.

He pressed his foot into the first step; the step creaked and he moved quickly to the next; he stood there and waited.

And then he heard, coming from the first-floor apartment, a woman's voice. Was he hearing a cry for help? The word *please*? He placed his foot on the next step; it made no sound; he stopped and listened. He heard again the voice of an old woman, which he knew now to be the voice of his great-grandmother, alone, no doubt, in her apartment, waiting for a plate of food to be brought down to her. Perhaps she was hungry, or they had forgotten about her, and so she was calling for them to remember.

But these cries were not from hunger, Tony knew, and so he slowly backstepped down the steps and stood outside her door.

Please, he heard again.

He unlocked the door and went inside. There were holes in the lampshades; the couch was covered with plastic; a walker stood next to the bed. The cries were coming from the bathroom. He found there on the floor, on that tiny part of the floor between the toilet bowl and the wall closest to it, his great-grandmother, two weeks older than ninety, her underwear at her ankles. "Did you fall?" said Tony. "What happened?" She nodded her head and said *Oh God, please*. He grabbed under her arms and lifted her onto the toilet seat. She made the sign of the cross. Tony steadied her and told her to catch her breath. She was holding her arm, and so Tony looked there and saw that there were no bruises. "You look fine," he told her, and she kissed her hands and shook them at him. *Gooda boy*, she said, and then she started to cry, and Tony told her to stop, everything was okay, she was back where she belonged. *Whata gooda boy*, she said, and again she kissed her hands.

Linoleum curled up from the floor. There was a stain in the sink where water had been dripping for fifty years; the mirror above the sink would not stay closed.

"I'm going to leave you alone now," said Tony.

No, she said. *Sophia downa here.*

"You want someone to bring you food? I'm sure someone is going to bring you a plate."

No! she said. *Sophia downa here!*

"You want Aunt Sophia to come down here?"

Sophia, she said. *Sophia for to help.*

And so now there would be no getting around it: he would have to go up to the third floor.

———

"Thank God for Tony," said Sophia. "Who knows how long she would have sat there on the floor."

"That's Tony," said Vera. "That's my grandson."

"He's done his good deed for the day," said Sal. "Now let him eat in peace."

"I can't stay," said Tony. "I came home to clean up, and then I'm going out."

"Going out—what?" said Vera.

"Where are you going?" said Sophia. "Do you have a girl-friend?"

"Leave him alone," said Sal, offering Tony a cigarette (the first from the package). "Can't a man have a private life around here?"

"Private life—what?" said Vera.

"What what *what*!" said Sal. "You're like a parrot." He turned to the others eating at the table. "My wife is a parrot." He offered Tony a match. "She already drove out your father," he said. "He went into the city to see about a job."

"Who drove out my Gino?" said Vera.

"Who sees about a job on Sunday?" said Sophia.

In the rooms were people he knew and people he did not know. Everyone had a plate of food. *Tony!* everyone said at the same time, and he waved to them, and they asked him how his job was, and he said it was okay for now, and those who did not know asked him what he was doing, and he said that he cut meat at the Italian deli around the corner, and someone said that was a good place to buy cold cuts, and someone else said *have you tried the potato salad there, they make the best potato salad*, and Vera said that their ham was not so good, and Sal said, "He's going to be the manager of that place some day. I'm telling you, pretty soon my grandson is going to be running the joint. Already they got him counting the money at the end of the day." Someone said that they don't let any slob off the street do a job like that, and Vera remarked that Tony had always been very smart, and someone else said *look at him, of course he's smart*, and Sal said, "Pretty soon he'll be running the whole show. They got good upward stability at a place like that."

"Let me fix you a plate," said Sophia.

"No," said Tony. "I'm just stopping in. I wasn't even going to come up, but then I had to come up to get somebody for Nana."

"Thank God for my grandson," said Vera.

"Your sister already said that," said Sal. "Does anybody else want to take a turn saying that?"

"Let me fix you a small plate," said Sophia. "Just a little macaroni."

"I want to get cleaned up."

"A few meatballs. What's a few meatballs?"

"I worked all morning," he said. "I'm tired."

"One meatball. Let me give you *one* meatball."

"Jesus Christ!" said Sal. "You're enough to drive a person crazy."

"Look at you with your plate full of food," said Sophia.

"Crazy—what?" said Vera.

"It would make your grandmother happy to see you eat," said Sophia.

"He just said he's not eating!" said Sal.

"Tony," said Vera. "Go down and sit for a while with your great-grandmother. It makes her happy for you to go see her."

"He's already seen more of her than he wanted to see," said Sal, and he waited for someone to laugh.

"I'll stay for a few minutes," said Tony. "But then I have to go."

"Where would we be without Tony?" said Vera, and she kissed him on his lips.

There was a snack tray with assorted nuts in the center—honey-roasted peanuts, walnuts, almonds, salted nuts, unsalted nuts, nuts that needed to be cracked open, enough nuts to make you sick if you ever saw another for the rest of your life. In the small rectangular compartments surrounding the large one were pretzels, potato chips, chocolate miniatures, hard candies, butterscotch suckers, raisins, and whatever else could be rounded up from the cupboards. So many hands had dipped into the snack tray that peanuts mixed with raisins, raisins with pretzels, pretzels with miniatures. "Do you have enough nuts?" said Vera, and Tony said yes, there were enough. She made sure the tray was placed near the center of the table where everyone could reach it.

While Tony waited for his plate of food, Vera brought to him a salad bowl filled with lettuce, thick slices of salami and ham, roasted red peppers, green olives, and chunks of provolone, and next to the bowl, on a small plate, she had arranged more pieces of cheese and extra olives, and next to the plate she placed the oil and vinegar for Tony to pour onto his salad. "There's extra cheese for you," said his grandmother. He ate a piece in front of her and she was happy.

She brought out some Italian bread for him to dip into the salad dressing left at the bottom of the bowl. He dipped the bread in front of her; she touched his head.

Sophia brought out a plate of macaroni covered with thick gravy, and on top of the gravy she sprinkled fresh parmigiana cheese. The macaroni had been arranged in the center of the plate, surrounded by large meatballs and pieces of sausage, and she brought out for him a small plate of ravioli (which not everyone had the chance to taste). "Let me get you another piece of cheese," said Sophia, and Tony said no, his stomach was getting close to full, he had plenty on his plate, but she went into the kitchen and came out with more cheese, and he said no, he couldn't eat any more than what he had on his plate, and she held the cheese near his mouth.

"How is your love life?" said Sophia.

"I don't know," said Tony. "Not so good, not so bad."

"Ask me how my love life is," she said.

"How is your love life?"

"Lousy," she said, and then she placed the cheese into his mouth.

The men sat in the back room and watched the baseball game. There was a snack tray there that had been emptied, and Sal called for Vera to fill it again, and she went into the back room to get it, and she stood there for a moment and watched them watch the game, and then she left. The women sat in the sitting room and talked about the weather—how hot it was, how difficult it was to sleep.

"The summer is no good," said Sophia. "So many children on the street."

"Children—what?" said Vera. "These are not children. They have the gangs now. They stand on the corner all day like a bunch of hoodlums."

"There are good boys in this neighborhood," said one of the cousins who was younger and therefore given to know such things. "The problem is when kids come in from other neighborhoods," she said, and everyone agreed that she was right.

"I saw a colored kid the other night," said Vera. "He was standing outside by the curb, and he was looking up into the tree. What was he looking at? What did he want in the tree? He was high on the drugs, is what I said to myself."

"You should have called the cops," said Sophia. "I told my sister," she said to the others listening. "She should have called the cops right away."

"And say what?"

"Say whatever," said Sophia. "Otherwise they bring their friends, and then what?"

"There was a fight the other night with a colored gang," said Vera. "How many times have I told Tony to stay out of that pool hall?"

"What fight?" said Sophia, looking now at Tony, then at his plate. "You got into a fight at the pool hall?"

"There was no fight," said Tony.

"I heard about it from the lady next door," said Vera. "She said there was a gang of colored fellows from another neighborhood."

"A couple of black guys came into the pool hall and then they left," said Tony. "That was it."

"As long as you're okay," said Sophia to Tony.

"It was nothing."

"I don't like this," said Vera. "This is a good neighborhood."

But what did *they* know of this neighborhood, thought Tony. They knew the market and the Italian delicatessen. They knew the price of chop meat at the butcher. They knew who was engaged, who was pregnant, who was sick, who was dying. They knew every crack in the sidewalk. But what did they *know*? The pool hall, for example. Did they know that there were fights there every night, always between Italians, usually about girls? Tony and his friends were just scenery in the pool hall—that much more smoke and noise. It was a beautiful place in a way—looking through the haze at a girl with tight pants and bouffant hair, the crack of pool ball against pool ball. Always there was a fight, but rarely were Tony and his friends involved. Two wise guys squaring off on the street below (even in winter they stripped down to their white sleeveless shirts). A fist slammed into a face, another punch thrown, blood on someone's shirt, a circle of *paisans* surrounding the fight, girls cheering them on (even the *loser* of this fight would be a hero). And it was hard not to be impressed by this show, by the absence of fear.

This was the neighborhood.

And the night his grandmother was talking about—there *had* been a fight in front of the pool hall: two wise guys beat each other bloody and then went back inside to shoot some more pool. And as usual there was the tension that followed a fight: the making of phone calls, more staredowns through smoke, the excitement (and fear) of not knowing when more friends would arrive and another fight would break out, maybe a brawl, and maybe this time Tony and his friends would get involved.

All of that ended, however, when three young black guys walked into the pool hall and up to the front desk. They wanted to shoot some pool, of course, but who knew how or why they ended up in this neighborhood. There were several tables not being used, but the owner said very kindly that he was sorry, the tables not being used were out of order. The gentlemen were welcome to wait until another table was free.

The fight was forgotten very quickly then. Every wise guy stopped what he was doing and stared, and the black guys stared back, and soon there was a change in their faces and they knew what this was about, and they said no thank you, they would come back another time, and then they walked out the door. (Tony could not help feeling a thrill as this unfolded: it was the feeling of being in a movie; even now, eating macaroni, thinking about it, he felt a silly pride for having been there, for having witnessed it.) The two guys who had fought just a half hour earlier went outside together to make sure the black guys drove away, back to wherever they came from. And that was how you became popular—you went outside to make sure the car was gone and everything was back to normal. If you did that, if you showed that you were not afraid, then people would say you were a good guy, people would know your name.

That was the neighborhood his grandmother would never know.

"I can't eat any more," said Tony, and Sophia told him not to worry, he could take a rest and finish later.

"Sit back and unbutton your pants," said Vera. "Let your stomach breathe a little bit."

"You need a good belch," said Sophia. "One good belch and you'll be asking for another plate."

"Hey Tony!" said Sal in the back room. "Come back here and watch the game with us."

"He's still eating!" said Vera.

"Let him bring the plate back here," said Sal. "It's the ninth inning already."

Tony left his plate at the table and went into the back room. He sat on the couch and reached into the snack tray. Vera brought him his plate. "In case you find some more room," she said.

"You won't be happy until he blows up like a balloon?" said Sal. "He won't be able to move."

"It's there if he wants it," said Vera.

"What a dumb nigger!" said one of the cousins. "Did you see what he did with that ball? He threw it right into the stands!"

"I've had enough of *this*," said Sal, and he changed the channel, and the others said wait a minute, hold on, what about the rest of the game, and Sal waved his hands at the television set and said he was fed up, the Mets were giving him a pain in his side, and the others yelled at him to put the game back on, and eventually he gave in.

"Who wants dessert?" said Vera in the sitting room. "There's cheese cake and pastries," she said when no one answered.

"We're in the middle of the game!" said Sal. "Bring it back here if you want!" He shook his head at the others and they shook their heads back.

Tony sat on the couch and loosened his belt. He closed his eyes and listened to the sounds around him—sounds he knew and would always know: a match struck, the rattle of nuts in a bowl, the chewing of pretzels, ice cubes dropped into a glass, the uncorking of a wine bottle, slippers flapping against the bottom of his grandmother's feet, the hum of a fan, plates being stacked, voices in the sitting room, his grandfather's cough, another match struck—

—someone calling his name.

He woke and saw that an hour had passed. Pastries were on the table; the cheesecake had been sliced; the baseball game was long over.

"Take a piece of cake down to your great-grandmother," said Vera.

"He just woke up," said Sal, "and already you're putting him to work."

"She's down there all by herself."

"She can hear us up here. She knows we're here. Where else would we be?"

"She's ninety years old," said Vera. "What can she hear?"

"Maybe she can hear *this*," said Sal, and he went to the record player and put on an old Sinatra song. He turned the volume very high, and someone said he was crazy, and someone else said why

not an old song, and Sal started to sing. He took Vera in his arms
and led her around the apartment, spinning her in place, then both
of them spinning together, and the rest of the family had gathered
around to watch. Sal moved lightly on his toes and Vera tried to
catch her breath. And then he saw that Vera was tired and he let her
go. But he kept dancing around the room, singing with Sinatra, and
the rest of the family clapped for him, and someone said, "Dance
with your grandfather, Tony," and Tony shook his head no, but Sal
grabbed him and held him close and led him from room to room.

"Look over here," said Sophia, and when they did she took a picture of them. "Now everyone get close to them," she said, and she
waited for the others to stand near Tony and Sal. "Don't move,"
she said, and when everyone was in the right place she pressed the
button.

The song ended and everyone said what a character Sal was. "Did
you see the way he danced with his grandson?" Vera said, and
everyone said yes, they had seen it: how sweet he had been—no,
how *fortunate*—to hold Tony so close.

He took a thin slice of cheesecake down to his great-grandmother
(he could hear the music upstairs, faintly). She had fallen asleep in
her chair; her feet did not reach the floor. Tony sat next to her and
watched her sleep. He remembered coming here to see her when he
was a boy: she was old even then, past her eightieth birthday, still
sitting in this same chair (though then she had been able to stand on
her own). He was brought to her before he was allowed to go up to
the other floors. Everything and everyone, it seemed, was brought

to her. And there he stood in front of her: she would look at him closely; she would kiss her hands and shake them at him; she would ask for him to be brought closer; she would touch his hair and feel his face; she would say something in Italian and someone would translate (*That's my boy, my pretty boy*), and then she would cry a little, and only then was he allowed to go upstairs (always there were new baseball cards).

She opened her eyes now and he showed her the cheesecake. She looked around the room, and then, as if suddenly remembering who she was, how old, she moaned quietly to herself. Tony broke off a small piece of cake and brought it to her mouth. She did the best she could with it, gumming it (she had three teeth left in her mouth, the family bragged), but some cake fell onto her lap. Tony wiped her house dress with a wet towel and offered her another bite; she refused.

She looked at him and kissed her hands. Her lips were moving, and so he moved closer to hear what she was saying. She managed to touch his hair; she managed to feel his face. And then it was clear that he could go upstairs again, everything was fine in the world, at least for this night: he was the boy he had always been, and who would know better than she.

There were still a few hours left of daylight. He took a shower on the second floor, washing the day from his body—salami and ham, cigarette smoke, sweat, his grandmother's perfume.

He left without saying goodbye: he knew it would be another hour with coffee and cake and more music.

He stood outside the first-floor apartment and listened for a moment before leaving. (There were twelve cigarettes left in his pack—twelve more reasons to be happy.)

Outside, it was muggy; already he was sweating through his shirt.

He drove to the park and his friends were there—he could count on that—but with them were people he knew but did not know. He parked the car and got out. His friends were glad to see him. Some of the wise guys were carrying bats, and he saw that some of his friends had them too.

"What's going on?" he said.

"We need you," said one of his friends. "We need your car."

"What for?" said Tony, and one of the wise guys said never mind, are you with us or not, and his friends wanted to know also, was he with them, and with this question he felt the night, all of it, and his life, the rest of it, slipping away.

Chapter Four

LETTER: VERA

(March 2, 1992)

Dear Tony,

Hello my boy. I say that because your father is my one boy and you my other. That's funny, I think. But that is the way it will always be.

But your father—he doesn't come around any more. What's the matter with your father?

You will forgive me for writing to you a letter when it was said by your grandfather that you don't want any. So I take a chance and write one. Your grandfather calls me a silly woman and I laugh at that. But I don't laugh at much these days. This is a very serious world. I say that to whoever will listen to me.

I made myself a promise. My promise was to say to you something nice about life. So here it is. I have noticed a few things about the winter. The other day I saw a man wearing sunglasses. It is not summer and so I wondered. Then I noticed that there is a bright part of winter, even during those short days, and the bright part is coming from the snow under your feet. Have you ever seen this? It is like having a nice carpet of very bright light under your feet. That is what I have noticed and here it is the nice thing about life I am telling you.

I told that to your grandfather. He said to me that he was going to bury me in the snow. He said to me that I should go ahead and open the window up wide and let in all the snow. You can see that he still has the same comical nature.

I find that it is hard to sit here all afternoon and write words for you to read. I have many words but they're all stuck inside my head. Plus there are certain words I should say and others I should not.

But sometimes I take a risk. So here is this. The neighborhood is no good now. Well sometimes it is good. But it is changed. Always they have it on the news. They say it is a racist place. Too many bad people, they say. And I want to jump right into the television set and show them how nice I can be. I want to show them how nice our whole family can be. There are two sides to every story is what I want to tell them.

Someone white kills someone black. Someone black kills someone white. And everyone cries out racism, and they like to trace it back to what happened with you and your friends, which I will not say a word about since this is to be a nice letter and since you have enough weight on your mind, and since your grandfather told me to watch myself, even though I told him we are family and there should be no secrets. So anyway, people in this city are killing each other. It is one person killing

64

another person. It is like a warfare. That is what they say on the news, and they like to trace it back.

There have been moments in this neighborhood. More of those protests. Don't buy macaroni at this place, don't eat supper at that place, bring your dry cleaning somewhere else. The neighborhood has changed. Too many people coming in from the outside. So now you know what I mean when I say that the world is a serious place and that I don't laugh so much any more.

But let me get back to the words I want to say and away from the words I don't want to say.

The other thing I noticed about winter.

Your crazy grandmother! She can't remember what was the other thing. I remember it was something nice. Well you know the other good things. Snowmen and all that. Your grandfather and I take a walk to the park once in a while to watch the children with their sleds. And that is the last thing I will tell you now except that I love you. People say things but you are my boy. One of my two boys.

Let me say goodbye. Sal is telling me not to write so much. He is saying something comical about my big mouth.

Love,
Your grandmother

65

Chapter Five

LIGHT

(December, 1995)

Vera lay in the dark and listened to Sal breathing under the sheet. In her sleep, she had been picking at the cut on her finger, and now, awake, she brought it to her mouth. She lay still in bed, careful not to disturb Sal, careful not to suck the feeling out of her finger, careful not to look too long into the darkness of the room, and how, she wanted to know, how could this man sleep so deeply, his chest rising very slowly under the sheet, how could this man dream so far away on such a night?

And what would Sal say should she wake him?

"Go back to sleep," he would say. "Tonight is just another night. Listen," he would say, "I told you Tony wouldn't come."

But never in her life did she want to be the only one awake. When she was a girl—could it have been seventy years ago?—she slept in the same bed as her sister Sophia, and always they tried to fall asleep at the same time. They had a system: they slept with their backs touching, and every few minutes one would nudge the other and say, "Vera, are you still awake?" or "Sophia, did you fall asleep?" Some nights they did this two hours, longer, one nudging the other, and in this system you did not mind if your sister woke you and you had to start over again, if you had to think again of the things that helped you fall asleep: the next day's lesson in school; how, on your way home from the bakery, you poked your finger into a cannoli and licked the cream. This was many years ago, but you will never forget—how you were asking Sophia if she was awake, if she was tired, how long before she would sleep; and then it was morning and your sister was next to you and you were not afraid, nor could you understand why a few hours earlier you had curled into yourself, trying not to look too long into the darkness of the room.

But what system did she have with Sal?

Vera sat up in bed. She saw shapes on the ceiling. She saw a face looking at her from across the darkened room, and so she leaned forward in bed and waited for her eyes to adjust: it was only Sal's trousers draped over a chair.

She turned on a lamp. Sal shifted under the sheet. (But would she ask? Did she have the nerve to ask?)

"Sal," she said. "I can't sleep."

"What are you saying?" said Sal.

"I'm not sleeping."

"Go turn on the television."

"I don't want to sit up by myself."

"Turn on the television. You won't be alone."

"It's too dark," said Vera.

"Turn on a light."

"I'm being silly again," she said. "Go back to sleep."

She waited a minute and then said, "Sal, did I wake you?"

"Why don't you have a snack?" he said.

"It's no good for my stomach."

"Have a cracker."

"It's no good. I can't eat this late."

"Put some cream cheese on it."

"I'm worried about the dark," she said.

"Turn on a light and listen to the television," said Sal. He turned away from her and pulled the sheet over his face.

She turned on the television but most stations were static. There was someone trying to sell her a mop. There was a rescue show about a man who fell from a ladder and cracked his head. And then she came to a program about the beach—small waves breaking on sand, the moon full above the water, a jumping fish. But this program, Vera learned, was *not* about the beach. It was about sea turtles. It was about a crocodile coming onto the sand and biting into a turtle. It was about the turtle being thrashed until it lay still on the sand. It was about the water gently running over the still turtle. It was about the next morning—teeth marks on the turtle's shell and its head missing. "This is part of nature's unending cycle of life and death," said the narrator. But there is a happy ending, thought Vera in the dark of her apartment. There is a point to this program, and it is about eggs. There are eggs in the sand! After such a night with the turtle losing its head, this program was about life! "But the danger is not over," said the narrator. Suddenly, this program was about vultures digging in the sand and poking their beaks into the eggs. The eggs cracked like eggs she would use for an omelette, and the camera showed the vultures with yellow liquid on their beaks. The camera showed birds pecking at the insides of the headless sea turtle. But this *had* to be about life, she thought. "Eventually, some of the eggs hatch and a new cycle of life begins," said the narrator. Vera watched them struggle out of their shells, legs short and floundering; they were no bigger than crabs. But here were those vultures again—snapping at the baby turtles, crushing them with their sharp beaks—and why could she not turn her face away from the television? Well, she was waiting for the happy ending—waiting, as the camera showed her the dead babies caught on their way to the sea. "Less than one percent of the babies make it to the sea," said the narrator. But here was one was making its way: it reached the water and dived into a wave (the camera following it under water for a moment, Vera waiting for a crocodile to swallow it). But this was all right. This was the life part of the cycle of life and death. The narrator ended the show by reminding Vera that this baby turtle would continue the cycle and would return one day to this same beach to lay her own eggs (and then the camera, for effect, showed the empty shell of the mother).

"Sal," said Vera. "Come watch this show."

But the show was over and the station turned to static. Sal snored with his head under the sheet, but it was okay—she liked that. It was the feeling of not being alone. She took this feeling with her into the kitchen and looked through the cabinets for a snack. Sal was right—why should she not have a cracker with cream cheese?

She sat at the kitchen table and ate a cracker. The cream cheese was cold and soft. She ate another cracker, and more, and one more, and they were not so good on her stomach.

"Sal, what did you do with the stomach pills?" she said.

It was fine that he did not wake; she could find the pills herself.

She ate one yellow and two pinks. Quietly she chewed them in the dark.

But why, she asked herself, must it be so dark in the kitchen? How would she see to make tomorrow's grocery list?

She turned on a table lamp. On a piece of paper she wrote: *eggplant, fresh tomatoes, ravioli, fresh garlic, one small sponge,* and then she stopped at the thought—unexpected, certain—that she was going to die this night. This thought was cold. It pushed out from her chest. There was no doubting this thought. But how would she explain this to someone? "Sal," she said with her hand on her chest, something cold pushing out from inside her, holding there. Her fingers shook and she went to the window and looked out at the darkness, at the fake light from the street lamp: morning, she thought, would not come soon enough to save her. "Sal," she said, but he did not move.

She went to the bed and shook him. "Sal," she said. "I'm not feeling so good."

He shifted his body and closed his mouth. (But how could she explain this cold that would not go away?)

"You must wake up!" said Vera, pressing her weight on Sal's back.

"What is this—a nightmare?" said Sal.

"I think I need a doctor," said Vera.

"Bad cream cheese?"

"I'm very scared. The room is moving in a circle."

"The room is just fine," said Sal.

"I feel something around my throat."

"Your hands are around your throat."

"I feel something inside. Something is going through me on the inside."

"Did you try a glass of ginger ale?"

"I saw a program about turtles, and there were birds pecking the eggs."

"Maybe you need a whiskey," said Sal.

"Take me to the sink," she said. "Bring some cold water to my face."

Sal brought her to the bathroom and turned on the water. "Give yourself a few splashes. Make sure it gets cold enough to shock."

"Is it cold yet?" said Vera standing near the sink. "Tell me when it's cold."

"There," said Sal. "That's good. Give yourself a shock."

"This is no good. The thing inside me is cold and now this is cold."

"What good is hot water on your face?"

"How long until morning?" said Vera bringing cold water to her face. "It's too dark. Never before have I felt this. How many times have I left bed for a snack? Never once did I have a feeling like this."

"This is some sort of nightmare," said Sal. "Give yourself more water."

He left her in the bathroom a moment and came back smoking a cigarette. "Is it all over with?" he said.

"Take me into the kitchen. I left a lamp on in the kitchen."

He followed her through the hallway and sat next to her at the table. He looked at the grocery list and reminded her. She wrote on the paper: *two packages of cigarettes, a block of swiss,* and then she removed the lampshade.

"That's too bright," said Sal, and he put the shade back on the lamp.

"I don't know what this is," said Vera. "There is something moving in my chest and in my neck. I don't have any control."

"I told you—it's a nightmare. Let yourself wake up."

"I'm awake," she said. "My eyes are open and I can see you and I can see my hands in front of my face."

"You have cobwebs over your eyes," said Sal. "This is a bad dream."

"I'm not going to make it until morning," said Vera clutching the table edge.

"Do you want a pill under your tongue?"

"No," she said.

"Listen to me. Make a strong cup of coffee."

"I'm too skittery. My insides are jerking around."

"Put a capful of whiskey in the coffee. That's all it takes."

"Nothing will work," said Vera. "I only want it to be morning."

"What's going to happen in the morning?" said Sal. "You'll still be here. I'll be here. You'll have the same jittery body."

"I want it to be light," said Vera. "In the morning, I'll have something to do. I'll have the grocery shopping. I can dust behind the couch."

"Dust behind the couch now if it means so much."

"I can't keep my hands from shaking."

"Give me an answer!" said Sal. "I don't know what to say. Whatever I say is no good. Tell me what you want to hear."

"It's too dark," said Vera. "I want it to be light."

"Here," said Sal, and then he removed the shade from the lamp.

"I want it to be light *outside*."

"What does that mean?"

"I don't know what I mean."

"You're talking nonsense," said Sal. "Listen to me. Have a mouthful of whiskey."

"Nothing will help," she said. "I can't explain it. I want to go somewhere where it's light."

"What do you want me to do?" said Sal. "Do you want I should fly you to China?"

"I think I need to see a doctor," said Vera.

"Go sit in the bathroom and turn on the ceiling light."

"It's been such a long day," she said. "So much food in the icebox."

"No one told you to buy so much food."

"How could I not have food? Tony would sit here with nothing, and then what?"

"Are you having a nervous reaction?" said Sal. "I told you he wouldn't come."

"He comes when he comes," said Vera (the cold she could not name flitting in her chest).

"I'm not going to sit up half the night if this is about Tony."

"I don't know," said Vera (the cold in her neck now, in her mouth). "I'm afraid," she said (and she could feel it in her teeth).

"I'm going to pour for you a mouthful of whiskey, and I'm going to sit here with you one minute, and if you do not drink the whiskey I'm going back to bed." Sal left the kitchen and came back with a bottle of whiskey. He poured the whiskey into the bottle's cap. He smelled the cap and then drank what was in it. "Do you see how easy?" he said. Vera held the table edge and that way her hands were still. Sal poured another capful of whiskey and poured it into a small glass. He placed the glass on the table near Vera's hands. "Go ahead and drink it," he said. "Pick it up and drink it quickly." He looked at her and waited. He played with the bottle's label and said, "Go ahead. This is only a nightmare."

She picked up the glass and smelled the whiskey. "In ten seconds, I'm going back to bed," said Sal. She held the glass near her mouth. "Five seconds," said Sal, and she held the glass against her mouth and tilted back her head. "There you go," he said. "Now you can see that it was only a nightmare, and this whole thing was about nothing," he said, and the whiskey was warm going down her throat and into her chest. "Now we can go back to sleep," said Sal. "You can have a nice dream and I can sleep."

Vera held the glass tightly. She looked at the lamp on the table. She looked at it very closely, and nothing could make her turn to look out the window and at the dark outside.

"You feel much better," said Sal.

"I feel better," she said.

"That's all you needed. You needed a shock."

"It was very warm," she said.

"Now we can go back to bed and you can have a dream."

"I'm not sleepy," she said. "Maybe I'll finish my grocery list."

"Don't forget, I want seedless grapes this time," said Sal. "Last week, I sat here five minutes trying to cough up a pit."

Sal left her alone in the kitchen. She heard the bed creak.

On her piece of paper, she wrote: *fresh bread, lemon juice, grated romano cheese, seedless red grapes*, and already she heard him lightly snoring.

She sat there a moment in the quiet and she felt better.

Then she felt worse, and worse, and much worse.

She went into the bathroom and splashed her face with cold water. She turned on the ceiling light and she was worse. She was much worse.

She went back into the kitchen and sat at the table. She read her grocery list from top to bottom.

But there was much to do tomorrow. For example, she could spend an hour at the store. She could dust behind the couch. She could polish silverware. Tomorrow, she could knit a pair of socks.

She held onto the table and waited.

The apartment was very quiet. She could not hear him snoring and she could not hear him breathing, nothing could make her call his name.

Chapter Six

BACHELOR PARTY

(July, 1989)

The naked woman was on the bed, and she had their friend naked very quickly. Tony's grandfather held his scotch glass tightly and laughed at the wrong times.

"When she's finished on the bed we should set her up with Pops."

"Let him drink," said Tony. "He wants to watch."

"She's getting paid, maybe we can pay her extra."

"He doesn't want any of that," said Tony. "Look at his eyes."

"He isn't that far under, let him take a crack."

Someone offered ten dollars to start a fund for Tony's grandfather. The girl rubbed oil on their friend, then she let her hair drape on his legs, and someone added five dollars to the fund. "Everyone chip in," someone said, and others reached into their wallets. Tony watched the girl lie across his friend on the bed.

His grandfather brought a glass to his mouth and tilted his head: all the ice had melted. His eyes were heavy and he was laughing at something.

"Did you chip in for Pops?" someone said, and the girl pulled and rubbed but could not get their friend hard. She used one hand and then she used both hands. She poured more oil and tried again. His friends were cheering him on, but his neck was limp and he was too far gone, and someone said, "Pops can do better than that," and someone said, "Who didn't pitch in for Pops?"

The girl whispered something in their friend's ear. He was starting to come along. But when she moved down and pulled at him it was too late. She gave up on him, and everyone gave up on him, and then they looked at Tony, who was the only one yet to chip in. Tony tried to rouse their friend, smacking his face and pulling open his eyes. He added ten dollars to the fund, and someone said he should pay more since it was his grandfather, and someone else said for the same reason he should pay less, and they left it at ten dollars, and the fund was up to ninety-five. The naked girl took the drink from his grandfather's hand and led him to the bed.

"Pull his pants down," someone said, but she was having a problem with his zipper, and then one of them went over and helped her figure it out, and then she got his pants down halfway, and someone said, "What size are those briefs, Pops?" and she pulled his pants to his ankles and poured oil under his briefs. She pulled at him too hard and he jumped back on the bed. He did not take to this. He grew angry. He pulled up his pants but could not manage the zipper, so he held them up with his hand and walked away.

There was an argument about money. Someone suggested giving her half the fund, but she wanted all of it, and someone else said there was nothing in writing and what was she going to do, and she said he was an old man and she was not a magician.

His grandfather stood in a corner of the room, adjusting his pants. Someone touched his shoulder and said he gave it a good try, and someone else walked by and filled his glass.

After a while he came out of the corner.

⸻

They took a cab over the bridge and into Brooklyn, the lights of the city fading behind them. Sal opened a window and breathed deeply through his nose; he spit on the floor of the cab. The driver turned around but said nothing.

After a few minutes Sal asked the driver to stop the car, and then he opened the door and leaned out of the cab. He stayed that way for a while—leaning over the street, his mouth open.

Chapter Seven

CIAO CIAO BAMBINO

(December, 1995)

But in the morning she was fine and she knew what she wanted. Her mind was very clear; her body fresh, her joints loose. She had never felt more certain than this, her legs never more steady—she knew exactly what she wanted, and who was going to stop her, who was going to say no, Vera, that is crazy, no honey, how could you think that, Vera honey, please, what you need is a nice long rest.

But how would she tell Sal?

Well, she would wake him (as usual), feed him (three eggs, bacon, light toast, as usual), and then, after he wet his hair and smoothed his mustache, she would tell him. But certainly after he stepped into and pulled up his pants, and after he read the paper. And of course after he watched his morning news program (the paper was not enough!) and after he went outside to smoke a cigarette (she would watch from the window above: the top of his head, Sal pressing

79

snow under his shoes, a cigarette cupped in his palm, never burning himself, and the smoke rising, especially in winter, so much steamy breath rising from his mouth but disappearing before it could reach her above, and never would she make a sound to disturb his quiet), and after he banged the snow from his shoes and climbed the stairs too quickly, after he removed his coat and sat in front of the television (sipping coffee, disgusted with all the silly programs, looking at the paper again, lighting another cigarette), and maybe after he closed his eyes a moment, maybe a short nap (the coffee cup still full, the cigarette ash growing then falling into the ashtray then growing again), and after he woke up and sat at the kitchen table for lunch, but not while he was eating, not with a warm eggplant sandwich in front of him, but certainly after he finished eating and put on his shoes and coat and went outside to smoke another cigarette (the top of his head, snow pressed under his shoes, smoke rising and disappearing, and so on), and after he climbed the stairs again (slowly this time), and after he took off his shoes and coat and smoothed his hair, after he sat next to the radio and listened to a sports show (the scores were not enough, the highlights not enough—he needed a three-hour conversation about a player's injured pinky), and after he listened and talked to himself and napped again, after he got up to use the bathroom, after he turned off the radio and stretched his arms and asked when they were eating supper—then, yes, finally, she would tell him.

But how would she tell him?

She had had all day to think; it was dark now and she did not know.

Well, she would think about *how* while she cooked the macaroni and fried the cutlets.

"Basketball is not a real sport," Sal said, waiting at the table for dinner to be served.

"You watch basketball," said Vera. (She turned the cutlets in the pan.)

"There are too many points scored. Am I supposed to care when someone scores one basket? They should start the game with five minutes left—then maybe I would care."

"It's a very popular sport," Vera said. "Is there a game for you to watch tonight? Do you want me to run to the store for some nuts?"

"I don't care about basketball," said Sal. "It's just something to pass the time."

"Your own grandson used to play basketball. Don't you remember? We used to watch Tony play at the park."

"Still, I don't think it's a sport."

"Wouldn't it be nice if we could watch Tony play again?" said Vera. (She poured the macaroni into a strainer.) "How nice it would be to have a little boy running around."

"Maybe you could put on a pair of shorts and I could watch you."

"That was a joke," said Vera. "You're trying to be funny."

"Football is the best sport," said Sal. "Every point matters."

"What about hockey?" said Vera. (This was an old conversation, and she knew her lines perfectly.)

"That's Canadian. That's not an American sport."

"What about baseball?"

"The regular season is too long. Everyone cares the first week of the season and then no one cares until the last."

"But you watch baseball all the time," said Vera.

"At least it's an American game," he said. "It passes the time."

"Tony used to play baseball," she said.

"He played in the pee wee league and then he lost interest."

"It would be nice to have a little boy who you could teach to play baseball," said Vera.

"Football is the only true sport," said Sal. "Sixteen games each year. That's it. Every play is important."

"That's not so many games. That's less you can watch on the television."

"There's no messing around in football. No funny business. If you lose one game, that could be it for your season. So what if you lose a baseball game—you have a hundred fifty more!"

"Football is too violent," said Vera. "Four or five men jumping on top of one man!"

"If we had a boy running around here," said Sal, "I would give him a helmet and teach him how to play football."

Now, thought Vera as she plated Sal's chicken. *Say it now.*

"I would like to have a little boy," she said.

"Go buy one at the five-and-dime," said Sal. "I hear they're two-for-one this week."

"No. Listen to me. I want to have a baby."

Sal did not stop eating his dinner. "Is this part of that nightmare you had last night? Maybe you never woke up. Maybe you need another shock of cold water."

"Why can't I have a baby?"

"Do you want me to call the doctor?"

"I know what I want. This is the only thing I want."

"Listen to yourself—you're an old woman!"

"I'm not stupid, Sal. I'm talking about adoption."

"Who is going to give you a baby?"

"I can still cook and clean," she said.

"You'll be two hundred by the time the kid goes to school."

"We have no one," she said. "Every time I think about the future, I see nothing."

"The three of us will take naps at the same time. You, me, and the baby."

"This is the only thing I want."

"I think you should take a pill. That will settle you down."

"I don't want a pill. I want a baby."

"My food is getting cold," said Sal. "Why do you have to have a nervous reaction while I'm eating?"

"Eat your food!" said Vera. "Forget about me!"

"This is nonsense," said Sal.

"That's right. Forget about the crazy woman!"

Sal shook his head; he cut his chicken. "Go ahead. Go get yourself a baby. But don't call me when the men in white suits take you away."

She remembered, before she fell asleep that night, what it had been like to have a baby. To wake early and see sleeping in a crib at the foot of the bed a newborn boy, and to know that it was her job to keep that baby alive. To nurse and burp and change it. To look at Sal and then at the baby and to say, "Look at Gino. Look at the baby." To let the baby crawl near Sal's foot. To bring him to the park dressed in blue; to sit in the shade and let people look into the stroller and touch his belly. And later, to watch the baby sleep at the foot of the bed, to lie on the bed and close her eyes and know that she would wake and hear him crying—and here she was, fifty years later, in the same bed.

Twice she had known what it was like to have a baby. She took her son to the park and let people touch his belly, and twenty-five years later she did the same with her grandson.

But when was the last time one of them called?

(She fell asleep with Sal's cold feet against her leg.)

She woke, moved away from him, and thought: *Now we'll see you make your own eggs this morning.* She washed her face and put cream under her eyes. Her hair had held during the night; her nails were not too long. And then she remembered—she still had her teeth! That was something she could say on her own behalf—they were not straight, but they were her teeth. She put on lipstick, encouraged, believing herself younger than she was. Her back was straight; her eyesight was good during the day; her memory outstanding. She remembered many different facts: the capital of New York was Albany; the F train went through Manhattan on Sixth Avenue; thirty days has September, April, June, and November. She wondered if they would give her a test. She could knit a scarf in two days. Once, when her mother and her sister were sick, she fed twenty people by herself. Yes, there were a few pill bottles in her medicine cabinet. So what if she needed pills! Since when did that prevent you from being a good parent? Her blood pressure was better; the large white pills were for her bones. There was nothing wrong with extra calcium for her bones! Half of these pills she did not take any more; she would not be lying should they ask her. Once or twice she had had a nervous reaction, yes, but that was life—who could judge her for that?

Her hair curled and sprayed; her nylons pulled straight; the shoe scuffs covered with a dab of Sal's polish; a silver pin on her blouse: Yes, Vera thought as she left a note on top of the newspaper, let him make his own eggs!

She walked to the corner, listening to melted snow run along the curb and into an open sewer. The sun was bright and she could see it working on the piles between parked cars. Ice melted on tree branches and water fell on her nose; she wiped the water with her gloved hand and thought: Let all of Brooklyn melt on my head, let the branches themselves melt on my blouse, as long as they give me a baby.

The bus stopped next to a slush puddle; no, silly Vera, you cannot ask for a baby with slushed shoes and wet stockings. She waited for the driver to inch the bus forward, and it was not such a risk to toe her way through a small puddle; the bottoms of her shoes meant nothing. The driver smiled as she showed her pass and dropped in her coins, and, what luck—a clean seat in front with empty seats around it.

"This is going to be a day!" said Vera, but the driver was busy with a transfer slip. "It feels like a dripping day, but that means we're through the worst of it."

The ride was smooth. Vera was careful not to be lulled asleep by the sound of bus tires treading water. But it was easy for her mind to stray; this trip reminded her of another trip years ago with the bus crowded and she holding a pole and her grandson holding her skirt, and it was easy then to think of the bus dropping them at the park and she making sure Tony was off the bus first, and then watching him climb on the monkey bars and hang by his legs and swing his body back and forth with his hair hanging down and so many metal bars close to his head, and she looked away (she trusted things back then: it was okay to look away, this was what boys did)—but what a fright when she turned around and saw Tony on the ground. It was the first time in her life she could not control her legs; she thought she had been stricken with polio. And now, as she rang the bell and waited behind the yellow line at the front of the bus, she remembered that Tony's eyes were open and she thought him dead. She kneeled next to him with her hands on his shoulders, and how could she not look at his eyes. There was blood on his lips and on his shirt; his shoelaces were untied (she should have tightened them before she let him climb on the bars!).

"Stop talking so much about his eyes being open," said Sal at the hospital. "Think about how lucky you are!"

"But he was staring up at me," she said. "You don't know what I felt."

"Think about his eyes moving and you knowing he was alive," said Sal. "Stop being so depressive."

"I thought he was mad at me and that I had killed him. Never again will I let him on those bars!"

"Everything has to be a soap opera. He's alive and everyone is lucky."

"I should have checked his laces," she said.

"I'm going to hear about this for the next thirty years."

"How was I to know he would fall on his head?"

"It's only a lost tooth," said Sal. "He has another one right behind it."

"I looked very hard for the tooth. I stayed on my knees and looked on the ground."

"Only *you* could turn this into something depressive," said Sal.

But today, as she walked carefully down the bus steps and onto the street, she considered herself lucky for having seen his eyes open. She had been through it once and now she knew what she should and should not do; and certainly she would tell them so should they ask. "Back then, I trusted things," she would say.

How nice that they gave her a cup of tea while she waited.

There was a young couple sitting across from her, a baby sleeping on the woman's lap. Now this, decided Vera, was an unfair advantage: this couple could bring in their sleeping baby and show how nicely they wiped its mouth and rubbed its back. But this was not show and tell, she thought; this was about who needed a baby and who did not. And if they wanted experience, she had plenty—Gino always with a fist in his face (how many times she cleaned his bloody nose); trips to the barber with Tony (the scissors much too close to his head, but she always held his hand as his curly hair—*beautiful*, said the barber—fell to the floor); and there was the third baby, crying for eggs and coffee, crying for the television louder, crying for her to shut her mouth. No one has more experience, thought Vera: fifty years of service, babies from three generations, and still she had her teeth!

She sipped her tea and watched the baby wake and grab its mother's hair. The mother held the baby under its arms and lifted it high and made funny faces, but how could she move the baby so quickly with nothing supporting its neck? Surely this woman had never found her child lying under the monkey bars; this woman's baby had never coughed too long or choked on its mother's milk or turned red from fever: there was no reason to lift the baby so high with nothing to support its neck. Did this woman know how easily a baby's neck could snap? And the father, too—half-asleep, reading a magazine. If asked about the proper way to hold a baby, she would say *always a hand behind the head*, and it would not be unfair to share what she saw in the waiting room—such neglect you would not see from someone with fifty years experience.

When she heard her name, she walked quickly across the room; she remembered to keep her back straight.

After Vera left the office, she waited for the bus. It was still morning, but the sun was brighter; snow piles were slowly disappearing from the street.

"I'm sorry you made the trip for nothing," the woman had said to her.

"Well," said Vera. "At least now I know."

But what did she know?

She knew that she could not adopt a baby. She knew, as the bus pulled to the curb, that it was okay to walk through a deep puddle; it was okay to soak her shoes. She knew that she was old: "Much too old to take a newborn baby," the woman had said. "But you have options. There are different ways to take care of children. There are nanny services. You can babysit a neighbor's child. There are many ways to give." *But I'm tired of giving,* Vera wanted to say. Her life had always been give. For the first time in years she was very tired.

What did she know after a morning like this?

She knew that she must ring a bell to get off the bus. She knew that the snow would melt and eventually there would be more snow and that too would melt and then more and always more. She knew the walk from bus stop to apartment. She knew how much a half pound of salami cost at the deli on the corner, and she knew how many slices to put on Sal's sandwich and how much mustard and how thinly she should slice the tomato. She knew the proper way to jingle the key in the door to make the door unlock. She knew how to take off her coat and shoes and act very happy.

She did not know what to say, however, when Sal asked her (not even a chance to find her breath after so many stairs): "Where is the baby?"

But what she knew, what she was very good at, was walking into the back room and sitting in a chair by the window. She had spent many afternoons with her elbows on the window sill—watching boys play stickball, waving to the mailman, counting the seconds it took a spider to float down from a tree branch.

"Where is your baby?" said Sal, who was smoking a cigarette behind her.

"I was at the store," she said.

"You went out looking for a baby."

"Don't be silly," she said. "Who would give me a baby?"

She waited for him to leave the room, and then she closed her eyes and listened to the snow melting.

Chapter Eight

SECRETS

(July, 1988)

He lost his virginity to a black girl he met in a dance club. He was waiting to use the bathroom and he saw her struggling with the cigarette machine, and so he gave her more change until the machine gave in and spit out a pack. She was very tall with light skin, and her hair was straight and pulled away from her face. When he came out of the bathroom, he expected her to be gone. But there she was holding two lit cigarettes. She was starting college in the fall. He was still in high school and would be lucky to finish. He was very aware that he was talking to a black girl, and he was aware that his friends would see them talking, and he was curious to see how they would react. He liked her perfume.

"You got a little jungle fever," one of his friends said, and someone else said, "Sure, it's okay to get a piece of that, everyone wants to fuck a black girl once, why not give it to her once," and another friend said, "Be careful with that, Tony. You don't want any accidents with that one. You might have to name your kid *Leee*-roy or some shit like that," and Tony laughed with them (even as he made sure to know where she was, who she danced with, who she left with).

He fucked her in the back seat of his car, and it was very hard to get in a comfortable position. She also was a virgin, and this made him like her more. They met several times the first week, and then every day the second week. They called each other at specific times so that no one else would answer the phone.

"Did you fuck that black girl yet?" said his friend.

"Yeah," said Tony. "Of course I did."

"Was she any good?"

"It was good."

"What did she do?"

"She fucked me."

"Did she suck you off?"

"Only for a few minutes."

"She has nice blow job lips, right."

"It was nice," said Tony.

"So what else did she do?"

"That's it. We messed around a little bit, then we fucked."

"You didn't go down on her, right."

"No."

"So was it better than with a white girl?"

"It was good," said Tony. "What do you want me to say?"

"You're going back for more. I can tell."

"I've been back for more. Where the hell do you think I've been all week?"

"So what is she, your girlfriend now?"

"No. We're just fucking around."

"Be careful with that."

"What are you saying?"

"Nothing," said his friend. "Do whatever you want with her."

She was very smart, he could tell. She made high grades in high school and would be at Columbia in the fall. He was good at telling jokes, and she laughed at each one and looked sincere when she laughed, and in this way she made him feel smart.

They messed around every chance they had. They kissed at red lights, which was something he hated to see other people do, and then she touched him at red lights and while he was driving, and then he drove with one hand under her pants, and when he parked the car they couldn't get into the back seat fast enough. They took off their clothes and he felt that her panties were wet and she felt that his boxer shorts were sticky and wet, and it didn't matter that they couldn't get comfortable. He kept his face against her neck and he loved the smell of her perfume and the sweat from under her arms and the smell of their fucking. And it was wonderful later that night when he dropped her off and drove home with the smell in the car and his shorts wet and between his legs sore. It was nice to get home and lie in bed knowing he had been with someone and she was still with him even if it was just his swollen lips and the soreness between his legs: he could stay awake hours thinking about what he had just done; in his mind, he could get into his car again and pick her up and kiss her at red lights and put his hand under her panties and feel the wetness there and look at her, and always the smell of her perfume and the sweat under her arms.

But rarely did he stay awake thinking about the one time it did not go so well: the night they parked and fucked in his neighborhood (how risky they became: once in her parents' basement with no one home; once in a park in the afternoon; but nothing as risky as his neighborhood), with nothing between them now, not even a condom, and he breathing into her neck and she into his, and the windows fogged with her feet pressed against the glass, and nothing between them yet never close enough, and then a knock on the window from the outside, and how fast she put on her clothes, but not fast enough with a flashlight shining from the outside.

"What are you doing in there?" said the officer.

"We're just hanging out," said Tony.

"Decent people live in this neighborhood."

"I know," said Tony. "We were just about to leave."

"Do either of you live in this neighborhood?" said the officer, and then he moved the light onto her face.

"I grew up around here," said Tony.

"You don't want me to wake up your family this late, do you?"

"No."

"I can very easily wake them up and tell them what I saw."

"No. We're going to leave now."

"I can give you a summons for this kind of shit, you know."

"We're sorry," said Tony, and he looked at her holding a pair of shorts over her breasts.

"The local papers check the police blotter every week," the officer said. "They love to put this stuff in the papers."

"This is not going to happen again," said Tony.

"There's nothing else going on here I should know about?"

"No," said Tony.

"There's been no exchange of money here?" said the officer shining the light on her face.

"No," said Tony.

"Good," said the officer. "That's nice."

No, he did not stay awake thinking about that night: how quiet she was during the ride to her house; how he kissed her cheek and said her name to make sure it was her; how he did not see her for a week; and how, when he saw her again, they did not talk about what happened with the light in her face, or about what the officer said.

But he could not get rid of that night. Even with his face against her neck and her bare stomach against his, he could never get close enough.

Tony did not stay awake thinking about that, nor did he think about one month later on the subway when two black men stood in front of them, one with a lighter, and said they were going to burn off his hair. He did not think about her looking down, he staring straight ahead, as they asked her what she was doing with a small-pricked white boy, look at his gold chain, look at his zipper head, look at that big nose, what, girl, are you doing with a *white* boy. They moving their hips near her face: she taking deep breaths and holding his hand; he making the decision to get off at the next stop. He would push his way through them if they stood in his way, he decided; he would grab the first one's balls and squeeze him to his knees, he would run onto the platform and scream for help—it did not matter if he looked a fool, it did not matter what bruises or scars he collected from this, as long as he could get her home and bring himself home, and then he could think about what this meant.

He stood up at the next stop and took her hand. They walked onto the platform and the two men did not stand in their way.

94

It became, like many things, something they did not talk about.

One month later, she started college, and that was the end of it. She made black friends who told her to forget him. Then she met a handsome black man who was very smart and who knocked on her dormitory door late at night while Tony was on the phone with her, and he knew she was gone.

Tony did stay awake sometimes thinking that she was not his first. There was the time in the back seat of his friend's car.

The prostitute had gotten into the back seat. Her eyes were very heavy. Tony's friend, whose name was Secchi (he had done this before), reached under her skirt. "I just want to make sure she's a she," he said. Secchi drove until they saw a gutted building with cracked windows. Next to it was a parking lot littered with garbage and weeds and pieces of concrete that had fallen from the building. He drove into the lot and parked behind a Dumpster. He turned off the headlights and let the car run. He got into the back seat. She put her hands on his face and then Tony turned around and looked out the front windshield.

"Is that all you want?" Tony heard her say after a few minutes.

"Not so hard," said Secchi.

A car passed on the street and minutes later it was back again. The radio was loud. The car moved around the block several times, and each time it parked outside the lot for a moment before circling the block again. Tony heard her in the back telling Secchi to relax.

"I can stay as long as you pay me, but not too long," she said.

"Don't worry about the time," said Secchi.

Tony heard them moving around on the back seat. He watched the weeds bend in the lot. The wind blew a plastic bag into the car and she asked Tony to put the top up. Secchi said he would be only a few minutes more, and it was not necessary to mess with the top. The other car was outside the lot again, the radio louder.

"It's not working," she said from the back seat, with Secchi under her.

"Try it with your hand," he said.

"I'm getting paid no matter what," she said.

"Maybe you're too tense," said Tony.

"Why don't you wait outside?" she said to Tony.

"I'm not waiting out there," said Tony. "Maybe we should give her the money and go."

"It's been five minutes already," she said.

"When was the last time you cut your nails?" said Secchi.

"I don't think it's going to work," Tony said.

"We're not paying her for doing nothing," Secchi said, and then he told Tony to get into the back seat.

"I don't want to touch her."

"It's a matter of principle," said Secchi. "We can't let her leave yet."

"I think maybe we should just go."

"Get in the back," said Secchi.

The other car waited outside the lot, and eventually they would have to pass it. Tony did not know where they were. Secchi was already out of the back seat, fixing his pants. He opened the front door and waited for Tony to get out.

Tony got out of the car. The fence surrounding the lot was very high, and the weeds grew above his shins. Secchi got into the front seat and rested his head on the dashboard.

"Can I watch?" he said.

"No," said Tony, and then he got into the back seat where she was waiting.

"Watch out for her nails. Don't let her scratch you with her nails."

Tony found a comfortable spot on the back seat and waited for his friend to turn around.

Chapter Nine

LETTER: VERA

(June 2, 1992)

Dear Tony,

Hello my boy. It is nice to call you my boy because it takes me back. Your grandfather does not know about this letter. He said to me I told you so about the last one. You know how he likes to be right every time.

So I take a chance and write another.

Your grandfather says to me that I am getting frantic. And when I ask him about what, he says to me about anything. I say to him that life is serious, as I said to you in my last letter, the one I hope you got, but your grandfather—he was never one to give sympathy.

I made myself a promise. My promise was that I would be honest with you and that I would not be afraid. But if you believe your grandfather, then you believe that I am very afraid of everything. So I take a chance and prove to you here that I am maybe a little bit afraid, but not so much that I will tell lies.

So here is part of the truth. Part of the truth is that I have been waiting for you to say something back. I understand that they have a way for you to send letters. I have taken your grandfather's advice about some things. He says to me that you don't want visitors, and I ask him why not, and he says to me leave the boy alone, let him do what he has to do, and I say to myself then that a family is still a family and why not help each other through things. I don't say this last part to your grandfather. By this time I have already pushed him to his limit.

But I will not take his advice about the letters. I send one to you and then you send one back, and in this way we stay a family. But it doesn't always work this way. For example, I sent to your father a card for Easter with a few dollars in it. Inside the card I wrote some words about this and that, and I said for him to stop by for lunch. But what do I get back from him? I get nothing from your father! This is not what I would call a family. And I say this to you as the truth.

Here is something else. The deli where you used to work has closed down. It makes me sick to think of it, and it is one of those things that gets me frantic. I thought that maybe they would have a job for you there when you come home. But not with all the people standing outside the store with signs. This gets me angry. And if you want the truth as I see it, I will tell you. They are trying to trace everything back to what happened. Always they must say it on the news. This was the deli where so and so used to work. So and so was involved in such and such.

I get a little bit frantic when I see something like that. And I would like to share these things with you, but at the same time you are still my boy.

Which brings me back to the other thing I was saying. The business with the letters from me to you. This is my second now. It has been three months since the last. It should not be very hard for you to scribble a short note to your grandmother. This is only the way I see things, and so I take a chance and say it.

This past Sunday we ordered takeout Chinese. I walked with your grandfather to pick up the food. This was not a good feeling. This was the frantic feeling I have been telling you about. There was nobody here for me to cook for. And I started imagining things. You know how your grandmother's mind works. She starts to think crazy thoughts. I was thinking that those people from the outside were standing in front of the house with signs. I was thinking that if they stood there long enough and said enough things and traced everything back then we would be forced to close down. The family, I am talking about. Just like the nice man who closed the Italian deli.

I have to walk two extra blocks now to get fresh cheese. That is something very small. I do not want to bother you with small things. But you can see that even small things can be very serious.

I have put here in the envelope a few extra dollars. It's not much, I know. If you do not see them here then they did not get to you. It would be nice if you could write to your grandmother and let her know.

LETTER: VERA

I am feeling depressive as I write this, but you have enough weight on your mind. I am good at bouncing back. That is the truth.

Let me say goodbye.

Love,
Your grandmother

Chapter Ten

LETTER: VERA

(June 4, 1992)

Dear Tony,

Hello my boy. May I still call you that?

I have been thinking about the letter I sent a few days ago. It has been said many times by your grandfather that you don't want. I have been asking myself for the truth about why I send. It is part one thing and part another. One thing is that you are who you are. My grandson, that is. How can I not send a few dollars? The other thing is that I have been frantic. I have been thinking maybe that these letters are to help me not you.

I was wondering what you think about that. Do you think I am concerned only about myself?

You may have read something in my last. That something

was anger. So I take a chance and say to you now that I am sorry. I did not mean to say to you about the Italian deli and who stood in front of it with signs and how they like to trace it back. That was just me thinking about me. You have enough weight.

I would like to say more about what is nice. Remember what I said about winter. Well there are also things about summer. The hours of sunlight is one thing I can think of now. The rest is stuck somewhere in your grandmother's head. There is more, I know. And maybe you can tell me.

Here I am, asking you to tell me. Here I am again, when you have enough on your table. So I say once more that I am sorry. I do not want to give impressions. That I am frantic. That things are so bad here where it has changed much. So I will say here for a good thing that I am alive and that every day I am able to do the same things I always do. I will say now that a few years is not such a long time.

I could just as easily say that it is a very long time, but I will not.

Allow me please one more piece of truth. Allow me the chance to say one more thing. Your grandfather, he is not so good. He never lets on, but I can see things. He mopes. He turns on the television, he turns it off. He walks around the neighborhood and comes back in a mood. And what can I do but place his supper in front of him and ask him is it okay? He doesn't like so much the summer. He is very uncomfortable. He goes through three shirts a day. Allow me this, since I said before the good thing about extra sunlight. This summer is not so good. Especially for your grandfather. The air is very thick in this city. But it is something more than that. I'm afraid that even my mind is tracing things back. It was summer when everything happened. But your grandfather, he never lets on. He tries all the time to be comical.

There I go again with the things I'm not supposed to say. I'm very sorry for the way my mind works.

Your Aunt Sophia, she is smart. She won't write. She says she knows how to leave someone alone. But she sees a pen in my hand and her story changes. Tell Tony that I love him. Give him for me a great big kiss. And so here I am, the bad one, doing what I have been told not to do. And besides, I told my sister, how can I give him a kiss for you when I cannot even give him a kiss for me.

These are long months for everyone. But I will not ask you to write. If I do not hear from you, I will understand that there is enough on your table. Some people need to go at it alone. That is what your grandfather says when he is in a mood.

So now we are straight on things and you know that you are my boy.

Love,
Your grandmother

Chapter Eleven

PROTEST

(September, 1989)

Sophia

They carried posters with pictures of the boy taped to both sides. The posters were attached to sticks they used to hold the posters high over their heads. Sometimes their arms grew tired and they held the posters low, and Sophia could not see their faces but only the face of the boy in the picture. Every picture was identical to the one used in the newspapers. The picture was a close-up, and she could see only his face and shirt collar, and this was how she would remember him years later when she could not sleep.

The family walked in front—the mother quiet and staring straight, her sons at either arm. A cameraman backed his way up the street in front of them. Reporters fought for space on the sidewalk.

Rows of police officers separated the marchers from the crowd on the sidewalk. The officers stood in a line and did not look at one another. A young man threw a bottle into the street, and his friends cheered as the officers arrested him. The bottle shattered at someone's feet but did not harm anyone, and the young man smiled as he was led into a police car.

A group of people chanted, "Niggers go home!" and some of the marchers moved closer to the sidewalk and held high their posters. Some people held watermelons above their heads. Some brought their children and sat them on their shoulders until they became scared and asked to be let down.

And how was Sophia supposed to get to the bakery with so many people blocking the sidewalk? All the way around the block she would have to walk.

She heard a boy ask his father why he was holding a watermelon.

"Because that's what monkeys eat," the man answered.

"Don't be silly," the boy said. "Monkeys eat bananas."

"Okay," said the father. "Next time they come we bring bananas."

There was a picture of Tony as a devil. A woman carried a poster with a picture of Tony on the front, and someone had drawn horns and a pitchfork. There was a picture like this for each of the boys involved. And what could she say about that? She could not walk into the street and stop this woman. She could not say, "Excuse me, but this is my sister's grandson."

A young man carried a bat and slammed it against the ground as he walked past.

A white man walked through the streets with his hands painted red. Someone threw a can at him and called him a "white nigger" and said, "Watch what happens the next time you show your face."

PROTEST

Sophia did not walk to the bakery. She stood on the sidewalk and watched the protesters walk past. She felt sick in her stomach. She thought the pacemaker in her chest was going to die. It was summer, but her hands were cold. She could not move from the place where she was standing.

The line of people kept coming. She looked down the street and saw the family getting smaller.

Sophia watched a while longer, and then she walked back to her apartment.

───

Sal

"Those people have some nerve," said Sal.

"This is doing no good," said Carmine.

"I won't feel sorry if they get themselves killed."

"They're asking for it."

They sat on a chair in front of the store and played cards. The crowd was getting thicker, and the people on the sidewalk were backing up closer to the storefront. Some of the protesters yelled into megaphones, but Sal could not understand what they were saying. A reporter held a microphone near Sal's mouth and asked him what he thought of the protest. Sal looked up from his cards and stared until the reporter walked away.

"How is someone supposed to get through all these people?" said Carmine.

"How many cards?" said Sal.

"Today, I'll do no business."

"If people need meat, they'll find a way to get it," said Sal. "How many cards?"

"One," said Carmine, and then Sal made a face and gave him a card.

A man threw a watermelon onto the street and the crowd cheered. Two police officers caught him before he could run away. They made him stand with his legs spread and his hands against a building. He argued that he should not be arrested. "They were looking at me!" he said. "That one guy wearing the jungle dress was looking at me, and then one of my friends said he gave me the finger." A group of people walked over to the officers and argued for the young man. "We're not the racists," a woman said. Someone else said, "It was just a piece of fruit." The officers walked away with the man, and the others stood there and agreed they should throw another watermelon into the street. "We should make them arrest every one of us," someone said.

"These people are walking on our streets, yet we're the ones getting arrested," said Carmine.

"This is why you never win a hand," said Sal. "Pay attention to what you're doing."

"I'm losing business."

"You're giving me a headache."

"I'm surprised you're not standing with the rest of them," said Carmine.

"Why should I stand there and yell back at them? They're a bunch of animals."

"They're carrying pictures of your grandson."

"Let them carry pictures."

"They're trying to make a case. They have all their lawyers pulling strings."

"Tony didn't do anything against the law."

"If that's what you say."

"Since when should you go to jail for holding a bat?" said Sal.

"Sometimes they try to get you for just being there."

"We have a good lawyer. Gino knew someone. We got him for a very good price."

"I would be a little worried. These things get political, and then forget about it."

"Are you trying to give me a headache?" said Sal.

"No. I'm on your side. I'm on the right side."

"You read too many newspapers."

"I'm just trying to look out," said Carmine. "I want everything to turn out okay."

"Look out for the cards in your hand."

Sal lost the next hand, and the next, and for the rest of the afternoon he had no luck.

Vera

She could hear it faintly as she sat near the kitchen window. A breeze came in through the window and blew back her curtains, but with the breeze came the noises of Eighteenth Avenue. It was much too hot to shut the windows.

She had not watched the local news in a week, and why not was simple. Years ago, when her son Gino was drafted to go to Vietnam, she had what most people called a minor breakdown, what her husband called a nervous reaction, what she thought of as a small death—a brief period of time during which she stayed in bed and accepted no food, during which she shook her head and spoke to God (so her husband told her). "And you did all that for nothing," said Sal after she took her first bite of toast. "They won't ship him over there when he's getting married. Your son is engaged to be married in a month. He was keeping it a secret." And so there was her first breakdown, and she thought of it as her *first* because, even now, years later, especially now, she was certain one day she would have a second. And for this reason she did not watch the news, nor did she read the papers, nor did she walk with Sophia to the bakery. But she could hear it faintly outside her kitchen window, and her mind was very tricky. Her mind was likely to make things up. Sometimes it did not take so much imagination. But I must not be so silly, she told herself. I must not let these people on the street make me feel sick and trapped in myself. I know that feeling. I know all about that helpless feeling, like a bug on its back. But what she was doing, she remembered, was protecting herself: this was prevention. She had daydreamed about this day: she watched herself watch the people walking down the street with signs and pictures; she felt her knees buckle and her eyes unfocus in the heat; she felt her throat close and saw her body fall to the ground; and there was more, her mind was very dangerous on a day like this: she imagined them dragging Tony through the street, his legs tied together and his face scraping the ground, and now, closing the kitchen window, she allowed herself to imagine this again, but then she shook her head and talked to herself and decided it was crazy—they would not hurt her grandson.

She played an old record of a man playing the accordion. This record had been lying in a cabinet for twenty years. She wiped dust from the album cover and from the record. It was impossible to hear anything else with the music so loud and every window closed.

It was a peaceful time humming these songs she had not heard in many years. She moved from one room to the next, and she imagined that she was in a ballroom. She danced from one side of the apartment to the other. It was very nice to know that she was the one making the rooms spin and that she was not a bug on its back. Her face was wet and behind her knees wet, her housedress clinging to her legs—

—but what a fright when Sal touched her back!

"I didn't know I was married to Ginger Rogers," he said.

"Dance with me," said Vera, holding his hands. "This is the *Ferryboat Serenade*."

"I have a headache," said Sal. "All those people screaming out there. It's like feeding time at the zoo."

"Have a dance with me," said Vera. "Please. I'm not ready to stop."

"Do you know what's happening out there?"

"The next song is a nice one. It's *Ciao Ciao Bambino*."

"I have a headache."

"Here, take my hands."

"Let go of me," said Sal. "Turn off the music so we can watch the news."

Chapter Twelve

THE CHAIR

(June, 1989)

They held her legs and the meaty parts of her arms, careful not to
bruise, and they lifted her from the bed in the first floor apartment
while someone held in place a hardback chair. Gino held the wrong
place, too near her elbow, and she closed her eyes and winced, and
someone said put her down, so they slowly lowered her onto the bed.
She wore a housedress and loose nylons. Someone held her glasses.

Tony placed towels behind her knees and under her arms and
made sure not to touch her skin. They lifted her from the bed,
pressing their hands into the towels so as not to bruise her or catch
a fold of skin between their fingers, and others stood close and
watched with arms extended, believing they could catch her should
she drop. Someone said careful, the towels were slipping from
under her arms; the skin below her knees turned white, and some-

one said wait, bring her back to the bed, and she winced as they carried her slowly the short distance and lay her on the mattress.

Someone moved the chair closer to the bed, and someone else said why did we not think of this sooner, and Gino (who was to hold under her arms) said he could not get close enough to the bed in order to grab her properly with the hardback chair in the way, and so they changed the position of the chair, moving it first one way, then looking at it and deciding it needed to go the other way, then deciding it was in the proper place to allow them to hold and move her in a way that would not bruise nor catch loose skin nor cut off the flow of blood.

They reached to the side and bent their knees so as not to injure themselves. Tony said *on the count of three,* and they took full breaths and Gino began with one. Someone held the chair in place. It was a hard back, but it was soft because the wood structure was covered with leather so it was comfortable under one's legs and easy on the back. The chair was very old, but not as old as its owner. She could not remember when she acquired it, and no one could remember, and someone said it was bought maybe as a wedding gift, and someone else said who would give a single hardback chair as a wedding gift or on any other occasion, for it was the only chair of its kind to be found in this first floor apartment or in the apartments above where her daughters lived.

They were bringing her, this very old women whose loose skin bruised and caught easily and who needed to be lifted gently, to the third floor apartment. Gino said *three* and they lifted her not so gently, and she winced and made a sucking in sound, and they strained to lift her over the chair and lowered her slowly onto the soft leather seat.

"Someone should bring her down a plate," said Sal. "This is too much work to get her up."

"You want she should sit down here all by herself," said Vera.

"She only wants to kiss the children," said Sal. "Let them bring down for her a piece of pork."

"That's no good," said Vera. "You want children running around with hot gravy?"

Tony said it was getting late and they had better carry her up.

Gino grabbed the back of the chair and Tony prepared to lift the hard seat under her legs, and there was no worry about bruising or catching skin between fingers; there was only the worry now of moving her through the open door slowly without catching their fingers on the doorjamb, and after that was done successfully, there was only the worry of not bending their knees and injuring themselves and perhaps dropping the chair.

They walked up the first flight easily, and she could not see where they were going (although she knew, having lived in this building many years, what the hallway looked like: one daughter's empty umbrella stand outside the second floor apartment door; a makeshift indoor clothesline stretching from one end of the narrow hall to the other—some of the clothing hanging from it her own). She could only see where they were coming from. People walked behind Tony with their hands outstretched to catch her should she fall.

The clothesline was the next thing to worry about: there was not enough room to walk from one end of the hall to the other and so no safe way to make it to the second flight to the apartment, where her oldest daughter lived and was now cooking macaroni and pork cutlets and where children and some older people (not as old as her or her daughters) were hungry, watching for Gino backing in with the back of the chair.

Someone was going to have to remove the shirts and socks and nylons and housedresses from the clothesline, all of which were preventing safe passage. Someone walking behind Tony (in front of her sitting in the chair) volunteered to remove the clothing and hold it in his hands while Gino and Tony passed on their way to the second flight, which led to the third floor apartment. Always on their way to somewhere else, wherever it was necessary to carry this woman. The man who volunteered could not squeeze past Tony, and his waistline (enlarged in part by this woman's cooking) would not allow him to squeeze past the chair. So Sal volunteered to perform the task of clearing space in the hallway and said that he would most likely hold the clothing since there were very few items and since they looked to be recently washed and therefore perhaps still wet and more likely to pick up dirt should they be laid on the floor; but at this time (shortly after Sal offered his services and just before he attempted to squeeze past Tony) Gino felt a sharp pain in his lower back and asked Tony to lower the chair, and they counted to three.

While Gino stretched his back and cursed his misfortune, Tony, in an attempt to save time and to avoid confusion, removed the clothing from the clothesline and passed it to the large-waisted man who could not squeeze past but who nevertheless wished to help, and he in turn placed the clothing on the floor near the umbrella stand and went back to his place on the stairs and waited, ready to catch this woman should she fall. But Gino could not continue with his back twisted into so many knots, and so Sal made his way to the front and became the one who held the chair back. Gino advised Sal to use his legs to avoid wrenching his back, and then he walked slowly up the stairs and into the third floor apartment where he waited with the hungry adults and restless children and gave them a progress report on the chair, now halfway up the last flight. The open apartment door was in view now to everyone except Sal and the woman sitting in the chair, who were still seeing where they had been and where they would go later on.

Sal could not see her face. He was very efficient, and it was a struggle for the others to keep up. As they reached the top someone thought that she might be sliding off the chair, but Tony said confidently that she would make it inside without slipping all the way off, and as they walked into the apartment someone said take her into the kitchen, and someone else said make sure the children do not come running past. But no one could squeeze past to warn the adults to watch their children, and so Sal shouted as he backed himself and the chair into the apartment, closer to the kitchen, but he was afraid his voice did not carry. He, like the woman in the chair, faced from where they had recently come. Tony and those behind him shouted for the adults to hear.

They reached the kitchen and they could hear children laughing in the next room, and adults talking about a football game on television, and they placed the chair in the middle of the kitchen, near the stove, where Sophia waited with a cut of pork. She kissed her mother's lips and then blew on the pork to make it cooler. She brought the fork close to her mother's face, and they waited for this very old woman to open her mouth, and Gino (who still wanted to help and who was disappointed in himself for not bending his knees properly) held a napkin under her chin to catch any pork should a piece fall from the fork or from her mouth, and the apartment grew quiet, everyone in every room now waiting for her to nod her head one way or the other. It had been such an ordeal for her to get to this point, up so many stairs, and it could take her a long time to move her head. This movement could be so slight, it was easy to misunderstand, and so they watched closely.

Chapter Thirteen

WAKE

(February, 1996)

Men in suits smoked outside, dropped their cigarettes on the ground, crushed them under their shoes. Cars pulled to the curb and people stepped out: men straightened ties and fingered hair; their wives and children smoothed their clothes and looked at the ground; the elderly struggled forward, squinted at the sun, reached for help.

He saw his father step out of a car; he saw his mother struggle behind his father.

Clouds came together and the sky grew dark. Was he going to stand on the corner all afternoon and wait for the sky to piss on his head, while people cracked jokes and looked at their watches?

Gino Santangelo was prepared to do so.

His stomach showed through his shirt where a button was missing. A front tooth was brown and loose. But there was something else: his pants were tight and too short: he pulled them down to the tops of his black shoes, but they did not cover his white socks, and eventually he pulled them up again to cover the space at the bottom of his shirt where the missing button should have been.

A priest arrived and shook hands with a man standing in front. He accepted a cigarette and together they smoked and looked at the sky. (When he spoke to the people inside, would he use the word *sinner*? That was the word they used for people who were dead and less than perfect. That's what you were the moment you died—a sinner looking for mercy. *Repose.* That was what they prayed for.) The priest pulled up his shirtsleeve and checked the time; he pressed his cigarette against the side of the building and let it fall to the ground.

Gino wiggled his tooth back and forth and a pain shot from his mouth to his forehead. How long could a person go without a trip to the dentist? He was tired of eating warm oatmeal and powdered soup, and when was the last time he bit into an apple?

Life was standing on a corner with rain falling lightly, then heavier, on his shirt and on his stomach where the missing button should have been. Life was a pair of pants riding up his ass and three toes sticking through holes in his socks. But life was exact and continuous in its imperfections, thought Gino Santangelo (if he tried hard enough he could rock the tooth back and forth with his tongue, shake it, manipulate it, until it was something hard and not his, a piece of food in his mouth, a popcorn kernel, and he could spit it on the ground, kick it into the gutter next to the crushed bird lying in the puddle by his feet, as the rain soaked him and made him retreat under the canopy of the payphone)—and did he ever doubt that he would end up exactly here, looking like he did, feeling like this, with the sky pissing on him and the body so close?

Even if he wanted to, he could not go inside with his pants clinging to his thighs. There was no room for even a wallet in his pocket. His glasses darkened in sunlight and were too large for his face. And what about under his clothes: the stray hairs that grew on his shoulder, his small prick. But none of that mattered, not really, for he had been loved (at least once), he married (once, less than a year), he made a child (who was now a man). But none of that mattered either: there was only today, this moment under the canopy of a phone.

———

But what would people say about Gino Santangelo, who stood on the corner, not far from the body, and pretended to make a phone call?

He married to avoid the draft and ten months later he had a son (whose cantaloupe head frightened him).

"A lovely girl," said his father at the wedding. "Look at them so in love." (Gino was not a coward: his father would have said that then, would have spit on anyone who said otherwise, but now—.)

He looked like Elvis (Gino would say about himself). He sang at birthday parties, communions, weddings—all the cousins wanted him there with his white suit and shiny black shoes. That was something. (But that was years ago, he reminded himself.)

Gino Santangelo was a coward with a big mouth and a small brain. No one liked him. People who knew him crossed the street when they saw him coming.

(He would say all of this before anyone else had the chance.)

Could he argue? He made it this long without putting a gun in his mouth.

Gino Santangelo was today. He was the next minute.

Did he want to be Tough Gino (walk into the room, ignore stares, say a prayer over the body, speak when spoken to, say *fuck you* if asked where you have been the past two years)?

Did he want to be Mature Gino (walk into the room, kiss your Aunt Sophia on the lips, wipe away her lipstick and say you are sorry for disappearing again, so sorry you were not around to help with the arrangements, shake hands, do not pretend to remember names, hug people you have never liked, admire flowers, ask children questions about school, say a prayer over the body and make sure it lasts at least three minutes, kiss her cheek, weep openly but not too loudly and not too long, sit with the elderly and hold their hands, say you will be there for the funeral, reminisce)?

Did he want to be Gino with a front tooth (eat beans and bread, sell your couch)?

He wanted to be but would never be. People could say that.

He wanted to walk across the street and buy a pack of cigarettes. Certainly he could do that. It was a start. It was the next minute: the first minute of new Gino (who did what he wanted and followed through). Perhaps he would smoke a cigarette outside with the suits, and, saying nothing, press a filter against the building.

But he was making no promises. He said nothing definite about where he would smoke—*that* was only perhaps. He walked slowly across the street with cold rain soaking his shirt and cars coming at him and splashing water on his pants.

He stood outside the store and from behind his sunglasses looked at a woman bending down to adjust her shoestrap.

He bought cigarettes and told the man behind the counter to have a great day (leaving two pennies on the penny tray). He lit his cigarette with a lighter rather than matches. That was something. (But his shoes were splattered with rainwater and another button was missing from his shirt.)

The next minute: a walk across the same street with smoke in his mouth (in front of the cars this time: they would not soil Gino Santangelo twice—Tough, Mature, it did not matter).

Was someone going to run him over?

Probably not.

But his stomach was wet and cold and suddenly he was conscious of his tooth: no one should see it; he was ugly and it made him worse than anyone.

———

Close your mouth, he told himself. There is no reason you cannot do this. Imagine yourself standing over the body and moving your lips. People will see your lips moving and will think you are saying a prayer, and why should you *not* say a prayer? Cover your stomach where the buttons should be. Breathe. Enjoy the smoke in your lungs. Do not think about the missing buttons. Do not think about the people who will stand behind you and say things you do not want to hear. There is no reason you should not do this. Rip the tooth from your mouth if you must. Do not think about the reasons you should not do this.

———

He went into the first viewing room, even though it was not the right one. He did not know the people in this room. He sat in the back and kept his face down.

A priest stood at the front and read from a Bible. He stopped reading and looked directly at the people sitting in rows. He placed a black tassel in the Bible. The lid of the coffin was closed.

The priest finished his prayers and sprinkled holy water on the coffin. He shook hands with the men in the family and hugged the women. He walked to the back of the room and out the door.

Gino waited with his head down. He stayed like this a long time.

People began walking past him and out the door. He closed his eyes and pretended to pray. More people left.

This was practice. Certainly there was nothing wrong with practice.

———

He walked into the next room and approached the coffin. He did not look at anyone nor did he care when he heard someone say, "Look who showed up," nor when he heard his father say, "I told you Gino would come."

The coffin looked heavy, and it was lined with something soft and white. Her hands were crossed and there were rosary beads wrapped around her fingers. The lower half of the box was closed over her legs. He watched her chest for a while. Her hair was in place, and it looked like it had been sprayed too much. Her face looked hard. They did not put too much makeup on her. He looked at her face a long time, and then he looked at the box, which was brown and had designs carved into the side. Her face looked plastic. This was not easy.

Her death was the end of something, he knew. He remembered watching her make homemade lasagna, laying out the pasta on the bedspread, cutting thin strips.

He stood over the box and moved his mouth; this was easy.

He wanted to know: Who made the rule that said he had to stay here with these people? Where was it written that he had to do anything more than stand over the body and move his mouth a little?

He walked in without a word. Surely, he could walk out the same way.

But he felt a hand on his shoulder. It was his father. "I told everyone you would come," he said. "These people, they think they have all the answers. Everyone knows my family better than me. This one says, 'Gino won't show his face. Why would he show his face after so much time?' The other one says, 'He's too embarrassed to show up.' And I told them, I said, 'Listen, I know my son. He's a busy man. If I know him, he's working on something. You watch, he'll show up,' and here you are."

Vera was crying loudly. "So quickly!" she said for everyone to hear. "My mother went so quickly! One day she was fine and the next she was gone!"

"She was ninety-seven years old," said Sal. "She didn't go so quickly."

"I can't stay very long," said Gino.

"Stay for a little while," said Sal. "Stay as long as you want."

"There are a lot of people here."

"It's a waste of money. As soon as you're dead, they suck the money right out of your pockets."

"Why does she need all those flowers?" said Gino (feeling good about agreeing with his father). "What is she going to do with flowers now?"

"This funeral business is a scam," said Sal. "Somebody wants money for a plot. Somebody else wants money for a headstone. Then you have to pay a priest to come and read from the book. I said to your Aunt Sophia last night, 'Give me the book. I'll read from the book. You tell me the page number and then we won't have to pay the priest.' These people don't understand. It's all a big ceremony. It's a big show."

"It doesn't look like her."

"They asked for a picture. The mortician says, 'Give me a recent picture of your mother-in-law so we can get the hair right.' You have to pay for them to make up the face and do the nails and set the hair. I said to him, 'These women spend enough money on their hair when they're alive,' but he didn't laugh. He's a real stiffy."

"That's a joke," said Gino.

"Of course it is. I've been telling it to people all day."

Vera continued to cry, and people took turns trying to calm her.

Sophia, who had been looking at Gino since he arrived, walked up to him and said, "What's wrong with you? You can't wear a nice pair of slacks to your grandmother's wake?"

"What do you think—people come back from the dead if you wear a nice pair of slacks?" said Sal.

"You should wear a clean pair of pressed slacks to your grandmother's wake," said Sophia. "Look at that—he has lint all down the sides."

"His pants are fine," said Sal.

"Did you see how nice she looks?" said Sophia to Gino.

"They did a fine job with her," said Gino.

"We were just talking about how much it cost," said Sal. "It costs a lot of money to look nice when you're dead."

"You should worry about something else," she said.

"I don't worry about anything. I want them to burn me when I'm dead."

"Do you ever hear from Tony?" said Sophia.

"I'm sure he's doing fine," said Gino.

"But you never hear from him?"

"I don't know where he is. I'm sure he has a job somewhere."

"He never had a chance to say goodbye to his great-grandmother."

"I'm sure he said goodbye the last time he saw her," said Sal. "I'm sure he gave her a nice wet kiss on her cheek."

"How many years ago was that?" said Sophia.

"You're like a drop of water on my head," said Sal.

"And what about *you*?" she said to Gino. "When was the last time you saw your grandmother?"

"Do you have kids?" said Sal. "Last time I checked, you didn't have any kids."

"You're a sour little man."

"When did you have kids that you can stand there and say what people should and should not do?"

"Let's go outside for a smoke," said Gino.

"The priest might come soon to say a prayer," said Sophia.

"You want me to stand here with my hands in my pockets?" said Sal.

"You need a good blessing," she said. "You need to get on your knees and take a good blessing."

"She was all alone at the end!" said Vera for everyone to hear. "She was in that terrible home! How many times did I tell her we would come for her!"

"I'm going to go outside for a cigarette," said Gino.

"Here comes the priest," said Sophia. "Wait until after he gives the blessing."

Vera was very loud, even as the priest walked past her on his way to the front. She said, "How many times did I say, 'Mama, your grandson loves you. Don't worry that he doesn't call. Your grandson loves you.' "

Then she saw Gino and walked up to him and held his shirt. "I told her you loved her!" she said. "Don't worry that you didn't call, Gino. I told her. I said, 'Your grandson loves you. Don't think that he doesn't love you.' "

Gino stood next to his mother; he had not seen her in two years.

The priest stood with the prayer book in his hand and waited for quiet.

"Don't worry, Gino!" she was saying.

"Everything is a big show," said Sal.

Sophia took Vera to a seat in the back and put her arm around her and rocked her quiet. The priest started the prayer, and Gino tried to move his mouth at the right times. Sal sat in the front row with his legs crossed, his fingers playing with his thin gray mustache. The priest bowed his head and raised the book, and then Vera started again, saying, "I told her you called, Gino! Don't worry, I told her!"

Gino stood quietly and walked to the back. He stood behind his mother. He was behind everyone now, and everyone was looking at the priest, whose head was bowed.

After a few minutes, Gino backed away from his mother. He walked out of the room and down the hall. He went outside and lighted a cigarette. He waited there a while, smoking his cigarette. It had stopped raining and the sun was out. When he finished his cigarette, he walked to the subway station and waited for the next train.

———

Two days later Gino sold his couch and an old leather jacket, and the following week he went to the dentist.

"How long has the tooth been loose?" said the dentist.

"A very long time," said Gino.

"Months?"

"Years," said Gino.

The dentist moved the tooth back and forth, and Gino pulled his head away. "I'm sorry about that," the dentist said.

The dental assistant had dark eyes and the skin over her eyelids was very dark and she looked sad even when she smiled. It was nice to look at her while the dentist stuck a sharp object into Gino's mouth. The room was very small and a light was directed at his face. There was no place to spit in this room. He did not see a small cup filled with water, nor did he see the basin in which he remembered spitting the last time he saw a dentist. It was the assistant's job to place a plastic tube into Gino's mouth whenever the dentist decided it was necessary, and it was this tube's job to suck out spit and blood and broken pieces of tooth.

"Your gums are diseased," said the dentist.

"How much does it cost to fix that?" said Gino, and the dentist laughed at this, but Gino did not say it with the intention of making anyone laugh.

He had been waiting a very long time to get rid of this tooth. He had waited a long time for this tooth to fall out of his mouth. He ate many candy bars, hoping the tooth would become stuck in the chocolate. But he had never considered himself lucky, and so here he was with a light directed at his face, and now he could no longer see the assistant, who, he realized now (the dentist poking his gums with a long metal object with a hook at the end), reminded him of his ex-wife, Josephine, who was dead, who he had married to avoid the draft, who would have left him eventually (he was certain) before she died. She had eyes that slanted on her face. Her eyes started higher near the nose and they slanted down, and this helped in making her look sad.

The dental assistant was whistling to the music coming from the speaker on the wall, and he was sure a person could not whistle, nor could she hum (as the assistant was now doing), if she was truly sad. Not once had he heard Josephine hum, and she did not know how to whistle, and there was one time he tried to show her how to whistle, and she made a funny noise with her mouth and spit on Gino's glasses, and it was one of their better moments. There was a day, not so long after Josephine moved back with her parents, that he picked up the telephone to call her, and dialed the number, and waited, and then he heard someone say hello, and then he hung up the phone, and he would always remember this day. He never spoke to her again. He never again picked up a phone and dialed her number. He was not good for her. When she was first sick he did not take the best care of her: he opened a can of spaghetti and cooked it in a pan and he called this dinner for his sick wife and his son, and now this woman with his wife's heavy eyelids was moving the bright light closer to his face, and he heard the dentist say, "We'll get rid of it in a few minutes, as soon as the novocaine kicks in."

That would be fine. He had been waiting a long time for this moment. Maybe they could sew a button on his shirt.

The dentist left the room. The assistant stood next to the chair and wiped Gino's lower lip.

The dentist came back into the room and pulled on Gino's lip. He moved his fingers around Gino's mouth and played with the rotted tooth. "This won't take more than a few minutes," he said, and he was true to his word, but during those minutes Gino remembered (and was embarrassed about his sentimentality) the silly look on Josephine's face when she tried to whistle, and it was a shame, he thought, that she tried it only once, and it was a shame that Tony never saw his mother make that face, and it was a shame that she never looked into a mirror and saw herself make that face, and he was losing it—he was concentrating very hard, he was trying not to lose this image of her face, but it was going (the dentist pulling on his tooth), and it was such a shame, he should have taken better care, and when he looked up he saw the dentist holding his yellow tooth, and finally it was gone.

The assistant used the plastic device to suck blood and pieces of tooth from his mouth. He was allowed to go to the bathroom where he could rinse.

The dentist walked him to the front desk. He said, "Of course we'll have to do more work. Your mouth is very diseased."

Gino made another appointment and explained his situation. That was fine, the dentist said. That was quite all right. And together they worked out a payment plan.

Chapter Fourteen

INVENTORY

(March 1996)

They were working inventory at a department store midtown. Tony had called his father a few weeks earlier: he was having trouble holding a job; he could not pay his rent. No need to worry, his father told him—he had connections. He was going to get Tony started. And now here they were, together, counting shirts. They were counting wallets and ladies' undergarments. Tony's father was showing him the ropes. "Make sure you take what you've already counted and put it aside," he was saying. "When you're done with something, you're done with it. You don't want anything counted twice."

They were working as a team. The woman in charge said at first that she did not want them together, but eventually she came around. "What is this—school?" Gino said, and then he and Tony were put together, one counting and the other writing down the numbers.

The store was open for business and there were people shopping. There were people rummaging through racks. There was one woman who was removing items from the rack just before or just after Tony counted them. She looked at the same blouse three separate times. "Hold on," said Gino to this woman. "We're trying to do something here." And then he was told by the woman in charge that he must not speak to the customers with such a tone. After all, customers were the lifeblood of the store. And what was he? He was (she searched for the right word) *temporary*.

"Please don't take any offense by what I'm about to say," she said, "but you and your son will be gone tomorrow."

"Hey," said Gino. "Some things you don't need to tell us. Some things we already know."

"I'm just making sure you understand."

"What do we look like?" said Gino. "Do we look like idiots?"

"So we're very clear then," she said shortly, and then walked away to check on the others.

Meanwhile, Tony was trying to figure out something. He was already on the next minute of his life. "Do you count an item if it doesn't have a price tag on it?" he said.

"Sure," said Gino. "Why not? If some poor slob brings it up to the register, are they going to give it to him for nothing?"

"What if there's no label at all?" said Tony. "Some of these things I can't even tell where they belong."

"Count it where you find it," said Gino. "It all gets added up in the end anyway."

They kept counting. They tried to stand in front of the racks whenever a customer came near. Everything was working out.

But there was the woman in charge. "You must not count anything unless it has the proper label," she said. "Did you sleep through the training session?"

"I'm doing it the way I've always done it," said Gino.

"Well for the time being," she said, "let's erase your memory of everything you've ever done. We do it this way now," she said, and then she showed him how to match one item to the others like it. She showed him how to make a label with the right price and the right identification number. She called this number the I-S-B-N. "Do you want me to put you with one of the others?" she said to Gino. "Maybe that will make things easier for you."

"We're fine where we are," said Gino. "Now that we know about the labels."

The woman gave him a look and then walked away.

"She's just bitter," said Gino to his son. "One time she asked me out, and you can guess what I said to her. This was last year, or the year before. Would I like to get a cup of coffee with her and her widowed sister? You can imagine what I said to that."

Gino had been doing this a number of years. He could not remember how many years exactly. Every year, it seemed, he needed to do this. This year they didn't call him back. This year he called *them* to see what they had. And he asked if they had work for his son.

"I can think of a better way to pass the day," said Gino.

"We'll have lunch soon," said Tony. "God, I could use a smoke."

"I can't wait to have a smoke," said Gino.

"Here," said Tony. "Take this shirt and make a label for it."

Gino looked at the machine for making labels. He looked at the buttons and the numbers on the buttons. "Listen," he said. "Why don't you take care of the label and I'll count a while."

Tony pressed the numbered buttons and made a label. He compared the numbers with the price and everything looked good. Around him there were other workers doing the same thing—most of them old ladies or high school students cutting school to make a few dollars. Around them were shoppers moving around the store. The buzz of the store was all around him.

The woman in charge came back to check on them. "Let me see that," she said, and Tony showed her the label. "You see that," she said to Gino. "That's the way we do it."

Gino made sure she wasn't looking and then he gave Tony a look.

"What do you do?" she said to Tony.

"I guess I do this," he said. "This is what I do today."

"What were you doing before this?"

"He's between jobs," said Gino.

"Too many people know about that," she said, shaking her head. "But this is something, this job," she said.

"I'm trying to get him started," said Gino.

≈

They went to the park for lunch—the park closest to where they were working. It was more than a few blocks of walking. The park was small with several statues and plenty of benches. People were sitting on the benches eating lunch. It was the first day of spring. This was according to the calendar. But the sky had not yet made up its mind.

"You know what that woman was doing?" said Gino. "She was trying to get inside your head. People are always trying to do that. They want to see your weakness. They want to know every little thing."

Tony was eating a tuna sandwich. He had asked for the tuna without celery in it, but they didn't get it right. He sat next to his father, picking at his sandwich. His father had a cup of soup. The cup was too hot, so he put it on the ground. "Watch out for that," he told Tony. "Don't knock that over with your feet."

"We have the rest of the day left," said Tony.

"The time goes fast," said Gino. "I mean, don't get me wrong. I can think of a better way to spend my day."

"It's nice around here," said Tony. "This part of the city is nice." He looked around him at the people in the park, at the men in suits walking along the street, at the tall buildings. He imagined all the people on every floor of every building. He imagined himself in the middle of something very important. He held this thought in his head. He could hear his father talking. It was slipping away from him, the thought he had. It was slipping. It was gone.

"You've got everything here," his father was saying. "You've got the park. You've got all these stores. You can get Chinese. You can get a slice of pizza."

"How much time do we have left?"

"We've got time," said Gino. "Don't swallow your sandwich in one bite."

Tony picked the celery from his sandwich. He dropped the celery on the ground and felt unsure about it. He found himself looking around to see if anyone was watching him.

"I've been wanting to ask you," said Tony.

"Don't worry," said Gino. "You can stay with me a while yet. Is that what you're asking? Because you can stay for as long as you want. There should be no problem," he said. "I don't see that I'll be moving. Unless this one thing comes up. You know how I get these opportunities. There might be something down in Atlantic City," he said. "I have a few friends down there. If it comes through, you'll have to find your own place. But don't worry about a thing."

"I was going to ask you how everyone is," said Tony. "That was what I wanted to know."

"The old people?" said Gino. "What do you think?"

"I was wondering."

"Are you kidding me?" said Gino. "Those old people, they go on forever."

Tony was holding his sandwich. He could feel that the bread was getting soggy. "You know they used to write to me," he said.

"Sure," said Gino. "They have all day to write letters."

"I was only asking how they're doing."

"Your grandfather—he's the same. What do you think?"

"I'm not ready to see them," said Tony.

"They're all the same," said Gino. "They never change." He lighted a cigarette and handed it to Tony. He lighted another for himself. "Don't worry yourself about it," he said. "Just get yourself started."

"Do you ever see them?" said Tony.

"I give my father a call once in a while," said Gino. "But your grandmother, she gets herself worked up. Why do I want to be around that?"

"How much time do we have?" said Tony.

"We have some more time," said Gino, and then he picked up his cup of soup. He felt the outside of it. "It's still hot," he said. "Do you believe that? The damn thing is still hot."

"Take off the lid."

"Forget about it," said Gino. "You think I want leaves and bird droppings in my soup?"

They sat for a few minutes finishing their cigarettes. Tony had given up on his sandwich. There was a young man feeding pigeons, and it was hard not to look at him: he did not look like the type of young man to be feeding pigeons. He had a bandage over one eye and a scar across his cheek. He wore a dark skull cap tight around his head. He wore baggy jeans, the belt hanging far below his waist. You could tell that he was big under his jacket. He was holding out the bread and waiting for the pigeons to come peck at it. He stayed very still and they ate from his hand. And then with the bread he led them to a puddle. He watched them get into the water and sit themselves down in it. Tony watched this young man watch the pigeons get themselves down under the water to wash. The young man got down low to the ground and stroked the birds. Other people saw this and crouched next to the young man, and he showed them how to stroke the pigeons without making them fly away. He showed a young woman how to do this. He watched as she moved her hand closer to a pigeon. He urged her on. And then, in what seemed one smooth motion, he opened the woman's pocket book, reached inside, and removed her wallet. He put the wallet inside his coat.

Tony finished his cigarette. He thought about telling his father what he had just witnessed. But then he asked himself why, what purpose would it serve, and he decided against it.

"Sometimes," he said, "I want to tell people."

"Tell people what?" said Gino, who had finished his cigarette and lighted another. He had given up on his soup.

"Anything I want to tell them," said Tony.

"So go ahead," said Gino. "What's going to stop you?"

"Sometimes I want to tell them what happened," said Tony. "Sometimes I want to tell them every last detail."

"Who do you want to tell?"

"Everyone," said Tony. "You know."

"You mean the rest of them—the old people?"

"I'm only talking sometimes," said Tony. "This isn't how I feel every day."

"Don't bother yourself with that."

"But sometimes I want to sit down and tell someone about it."

"Don't worry yourself," said Gino.

"It doesn't have to be them," said Tony. "It could be anybody."

"Get yourself straight first. You need to get your bearings."

"I would like to tell someone the whole thing, and that I'm not such an angel."

"You don't need to say anything," said Gino. "You're just getting yourself started."

"I'm no angel, you know. Someone should tell them once in a while that I'm not an angel."

"That's all right," said Gino. "It's okay to feel that way." He stood up and looked at his watch. He threw his cigarette onto the ground.

"Do we have to go back now?" said Tony.

"We should get back."

The young man was feeding pigeons again, and different people were going over to watch him. It was the first day of spring, but the sky was turning dark. The sky could not make up its mind.

Gino was looking at his watch. He was looking at his son.

"Are you sure we don't have any more time?" said Tony. "Are you sure we don't have a few minutes more?"

Chapter Fifteen

LETTER: SOPHIA

(December 10, 1992)

Dear Tony,

Your grandmother is asking me to write to you on account of you not writing back in so long, but don't let on please that I am telling you what's what. She has been taken ill to the bed for a few days now. I think it was Thanksgiving that did it to her. The reason being that nobody was here. We had a small bird for the three of us. Not even your father. But just between you and me, I say that this is none of your business. You have your own business. No one's here for turkey dinner and she starts crying about her boy, her Tony. Everything changed when he went away, she is crying. This is our penance, she is saying. And right away she tells me to send you a letter. Tell him to write to me, she is saying. And what am I supposed to do when she hands me a pen and paper? I know what you said about not wanting anything. No visitors, no letters, no nothing. So that's the way you should have it, is what I say. But on account of your grandmother being laid up in bed, and also on account that she handed me the pen and paper, here is a letter to you asking I don't know what. For what should I ask? I should ask for a new pair of legs. Can you give me that? Or maybe you can give me young hands? (This is just your Aunt Sophia being funny.) I asked your grandfather should I say hello to you from him, and he gives me a look. So I am saying hello anyway. Now, on account that I have a pen in my hand, let me ask if you could send your grandmother a few words before the holiday. This is not coming from me. You know how I feel about whose business is whose business. This request is only on account that she asked me and because she is your grandmother, and also because she is laid up. She is crying all the time that the rooms are too empty. It's like a funeral parlor even on Sunday, she is saying. One day everything will be gone, she says. We all have our ups and our downs, I tell her. This is the only letter I am writing to you. The reason being that you don't want any. I hope you are having an up not a down. This is the last thing I will say.

Love and kisses,
Aunt Sophia

Chapter Sixteen

A FINE PLACE

(December, 1996)

"Martha," said Vera to the nurse. "My husband said for me to give you this." She held in her hand a five dollar bill. "I talked with my husband last night, after you left, and he said to me, 'You should give the nurse some extra money for car fare. You know she's working for much less than you would pay someone else,' he said, and I said to myself, 'Vera, he's right. Martha is very good to you. She has three small children and she cleans your dishes and she goes to the market'—and I don't mind that you came back yesterday with the wrong fish, it was silly of me to care about such a thing, and I told my husband, I said, 'I don't care that Martha came back with the wrong fish. Fish is fish. It all goes down,' and he agreed with me, and that was when he said, 'Are you crazy? You should give her something extra.' This is my husband's money, of course. When he said I should give to you something extra, he didn't mean for me to give you out of my own money. He gives me money for things like this. So I said to myself this morning—this was early, before you came, when the other nurse was here—she's a young black woman, she's a very big woman, and sometimes I'm not so sure she hears what I say, you know, she might not be so good with the language, like when I ask her to change the television station she sometimes changes the bed sheets, and I never send her to the market, who knows what she'll bring back, but I have you for that, whenever I think of sending her to the market, I say to myself, 'No, you can wait. You have Martha. Why do you need fish right now? You can send Martha when she gets here'—but this morning I said to myself, 'Vera. Silly Vera. You must remember to give something extra to Martha for all her hard work.' But I'll tell you something else my husband said—he's down at the butcher shop today with his friends, every Sunday morning he goes. He got very angry with me. I told him how I asked you to wash the floors the other day. I told him, 'Martha was here and she made a lunch for me, and I asked her to eat with me, but she did not want anything'—do you remember that, when I asked you and you said no, you did not want anything, you said, 'Please, Vera. Take care of yourself. Feed your own bones.' I remember that—what you said about feeding my bones. I remember it because my bones don't feel so good, and the pain in my side gets better and then it gets worse. I had a full week with no pain, but then it comes again and I get afraid. You've seen me afraid. I said to my husband, 'Martha has seen me afraid. She knows how I get,' and I say this to him because he gets angry at me, he tells me to stay calm, and I really do have a bad habit of getting upset, but you know that, and that's what I tell my husband, I say, 'Martha knows what to do when I get upset. You're at the butcher every day now, not just Sunday.' And this, my husband says, is why

I should give you a little extra. But he got angry with me. That's what I was telling you. I told him how we finished lunch and that you did not want anything, and then I looked at the floor and thought that it would be nice if I could clean the floor, if my side did not hurt so much that it made it impossible to get down on my hands and knees and wash the floor, and I was very sad to be stuck in this chair—you know how I get, Martha, you've seen me at my worst—and I said to myself, 'Now why would Martha not want to help you with this little thing, this spot on the floor?' and that was when I asked you, and I asked you nicely—please tell me if I did not ask you nicely—I said, 'Martha, would you mind washing the floor?' and you said yes and I was very happy, but I can tell you now, and I have told you before, that I did not expect you to go to the store for a new mop. I did not know I was missing my mop—but now I remember, I was using it to shoo away a bird from my fire escape and I dropped it onto the street, and then I said, 'Who's going to walk down a flight of stairs just for a mop?' And you said you did not mind walking to the store, and you did a good job with that, you bought the same mop I always use, and so I was telling my husband about this, how I asked you to clean the floor, and what does he say? He says, 'Are you crazy? You don't ask a nurse to wash the floor!' His voice was very loud. My husband is a nice man, everyone likes him. People say, 'Your husband is a nice man, he has many friends,' and I say, 'He takes good care of me. I give him a headache but he takes good care.' This is what I tell people so they know what my husband is like. But I think, sometimes, that I get him angry. Like this time I'm telling you about—if you could have heard the tone to his voice! 'These people are there to take care of you in case of an emergency,' he said to me. 'These women are nurses, not maids!' And I said, 'Who's a maid? Who said Martha is a maid?' And he said, 'These women are getting paid very little money to help you. Do you know what it means to pay someone off the books?' That's what he said to me. What do I know about off the books? You pay someone—that's all I know. 'Martha is taking a cab here every day,' my husband said to me. 'Did you know every day she's paying for a cab to see you?' But what do I know? I see buses on the street. I think that people take the bus. But my husband set me straight. He said, 'This is how we do things. This is how normal people do things.' So here, Martha—I'm giving you a little extra today. I didn't know about off the books and I look out the window and I see a bus go down the street. So here—take this," said Vera giving the money to Martha. "But the other thing my husband said," said Vera—and this thought made her so happy she almost gave Martha another dollar—"he said he was going to stay home tomorrow. He's going to take a day away from his friends and stay home with me. He wants to make sure everything is okay."

Vera had not left Sophia's apartment in three days, but Sophia was determined to get her out. She had had enough of her sister's moaning at every pain. And what could *she* do—her own pacemaker was fourteen years old! Three weeks, Sal paid for nurses, but then he said he couldn't afford them. Someone had to take care of Vera. But surely Vera did not expect Sophia to give her a bath. She did that not even for her mother, who died in a rest home.

It was almost four o'clock and still Vera snored on the bed. Wind pressed against the windows and shook the glass.

They fought each night for space on the bed. Every day the sheets were changed.

144

And where was Vera's son? Where was her grandson? Where was her husband?

Sal sat downstairs watching the football game. He showed his face every few hours to ask questions. "Is she comfortable?" he would ask Sophia, but never would he say to his wife, *I love you. I will be lost without you.* Why should he lie?

⸻

Vera opened her eyes and saw Sophia standing above her with a cup of hot tea (with honey, she hoped). "My legs," said Vera. "Move the covers so I can see them."

Sophia placed the cup on the table next to the bed. "I wish you would stop looking at yourself."

"My poor legs," said Vera. "So heavy."

Sophia pulled back the sheets and blankets and looked away when she saw that Vera's legs were getting bigger.

"But the doctor was such a nice young man," said Vera. "What went wrong?"

"We're going for a walk today," said Sophia. "The church is only a few blocks away."

"This is how it all begins," Vera said.

"Stop your nonsense," said Sophia. She held the cup near Vera's mouth.

"Why is God giving me this?" said Vera, and then she blew on the hot cup.

"Be quiet or I'll put you out on the sidewalk," said Sophia.

The cup was much too hot. Sophia took away the cup and left Vera alone in the darkening room. There were too many shadows on the ceiling. Vera would not admit this to anyone, not even to her sister, but she was looking for her mother on the ceiling: someone to come and stop the swelling in her legs, an angel who would float above the bed and reach down inside her to fix the problem.

She struggled to the edge of the bed but the floor was too far away. She covered her legs and waited.

＝

"This is how people die," Vera said (with hot oatmeal on her chin).

"When are you going to stop?" said Sophia. She pulled up Vera's nylons.

"I'm stuck," said Vera. "This is how it starts."

"Enough," said Sophia, and it occurred to her that she had never watched someone die. She watched her husband die, yes—she saw the cancer eat him from the inside until he disappeared—but she was not there when he breathed out and made his hands into fists (she imagined) and did not breathe in again. She had wanted to be there. She told her sister and her mother and she promised her husband— she wanted to hold his hand and take him through it.

He lived in flannel pajamas for the last month. He was always under a blanket.

She found him cold and staring at the ceiling, and she did not want to pull back the sheets to find what could be there: what she had been told was there when someone died: the mess of death, the smell of it.

(Vera brought rosary beads and stayed in the kitchen. Sal sat on the edge of the bed and closed the eyes. Sophia looked and the sheets were white.)

＝

Vera tried to push her swollen feet into shoes. She pushed and got them so far and stopped for breath. Her stomach tightened and the room grew dark and the knot in her stomach pulled and twisted around itself. Her legs dangled off the side of the bed. The pain in her side was back, a dull ache that came and went and scared her to tears. Three weeks ago the doctor sent her home with a bottle of pills, and what good did they do? All the tests they ran! And for what—a body filled with water and a squeezing pain in her side? Shadows moved above her and the ceiling darkened and the shadows disappeared.

"What good were the tests?" said Vera for Sophia to hear in the kitchen.

There came no answer. Vera stretched her toes and reached the shoes and again tried to squeeze her feet into them.

"Why am I not getting better?" said Vera, and again she heard no answer. The pain gripped her side and she moaned for Sophia to hear.

"What happened?" said Sophia walking into the bedroom.

"My side," said Vera holding her side.

"You have a pain?" said Sophia.

"The doctor seemed like a nice young man," said Vera before she moaned again.

"You had a gallstone removed," said Sophia. "It's normal to have pain."

"I'm no better."

"It takes time," said Sophia (on her knee, stretching a shoe).

"I had the pain *before* I went into the hospital," said Vera.

"Give it time!" said Sophia.

"All those tests for what?" said Vera

"Stop being such a baby!"

147

"Every night I say a prayer."

"You need to get outside," said Sophia trying to fit Vera's foot into a shoe.

"This is no good," said Vera. "Where is Sal?"

"I'll get a pair of slippers."

"Slippers on the ice!"

"You need to get out!" said Sophia before she left the room.

"I'll never leave this room," said Vera by herself in the quiet darkening bedroom. "This is the beginning," said Vera for Sophia to hear.

Sophia covered her sister's feet with thick socks and pushed them into a pair of slippers. Vera shuffled slowly across the room holding her side. Sophia put on her coat and looked out the window. Wind knocked branches from trees; people walked gingerly over ice. A street light came on.

A walk around the block will be enough, thought Sophia—and where was Sal at a time like this?

"What happens when she doesn't get better?" Sophia had asked him.

"We'll tell her eventually," he said.

"You will tell her."

"Not yet," he said.

"People are not stupid," said Sophia.

"You saw how she was with the breast cancer—she was ready to kill herself!"

"She screamed a little bit," said Sophia. "That was almost twenty years ago."

"She was hysterical."

"Someone shouldn't get upset when they have cancer?"

"You know how your sister is—she gives up."

"This is terminal," said Sophia. "What is there to give up?"

"Let her enjoy the next few months," he said, but now it was weeks later and where was *he* when his wife's legs were blowing up?

Vera stood next to the bed with a coat at her feet. Sophia picked up the coat and tried to give it to Vera but she would not take it. She sat on the bed and let the slippers fall off her feet. "I can't leave the apartment," she said.

"Just for a walk," said Sophia. "We'll hold hands."

"I can't leave," she said. "Where is my Sal?"

"Ten minutes," said Sophia. "You need the air."

"I'm afraid I'll never leave," said Vera.

"We'll go right now," said Sophia.

"I'm afraid."

"What is going to happen?" said Sophia.

"I can't move."

"What is going to happen outside?"

"I won't make it back."

"But you're afraid you'll never leave."

"My legs," said Vera.

"Your legs are fine," said Sophia. "You can hold my hand."

"I can't do it," said Vera.

"What happened?" said Sophia. "We had the slippers on your feet."

"I'll never leave this room."

"You *will* leave this room."

"It's getting darker," said Vera. "I need to see."

"You can see," said Sophia.

"Turn on a lamp."

"I have the lamp on."

"Another one," said Vera.

Sophia turned on a second lamp but the bulb blew and Vera let out a short cry.

"Let me put your slippers on," said Sophia.

"I can't."

"Let me get you something to eat."

"I can't eat."

"You *can*," said Sophia.

"I want to stay here," said Vera. "Let me stay for now."

The room was becoming too familiar. Vera lay on the bed and she knew the shapes of all the shadows on the ceiling. She knew the red pen sitting on the desk across from the bed; she knew the finger smudges on the body length mirror on the closet door; she knew how many seconds passed between waves of pain in her side; she knew where the small hand and big hand were stopped on the clock shaped like a baseball on the desk across from the bed.

She listened for heartbeats and thought, after hearing the clock instead, that this bed was not a fine place to die. She would never leave and she must find a place in this apartment: a place where the shadows were not shaped like long fingers and did not reach for her. A bed was fine for her mother, a hard bed in a rest home, but she wanted something else—and how long she had gone without a warm bath. She was sick of sponge baths: it gave her a chill when the water ran down her body and off her legs and into the dry tub. Sitting in a bath would be a fine way to die, with an endless supply of hot water to add if the water got cold, with bubbles covering the old and purple scar under her arm. She was going to pass each moment in a fine place, she decided. (But she did not want to die.) She would try always to be in the middle of something. She would spend her time counting bubbles and popping them and warming the water in the tub, and she would have little time to bother with shadows. Under the water her legs could be thin again, and who could ask for a finer place? How could a body grow cold under so much hot water? She sat up in bed and called for Sophia.

Sophia held her hands under the faucet; hot water dripped from her hands and into the tub. The walls were starting to sweat.

She found Vera talking to herself in bed.

"I was praying," said Vera.

"Pray for me," said Sophia.

"I always pray for others," said Vera (who had been wishing away her swollen legs).

Sophia pulled Vera from the bed and they walked slowly across the room. "Now I put my left foot forward," said Vera with every other step.

Sophia lifted a red sweater over her sister's head. She unzippered a skirt and pulled it down and removed the rest gently until the clothes piled at Vera's feet. The mirror steamed and bubbles rose over the sides of the tub. Sophia turned off the water with her sweaty hand.

This was the bathroom where Vera hid and cried one year ago, Sophia remembered, when Tony did not come home. "You'll never learn," Sal had said to Vera. "You'll never see your grandson again." And then Vera ran out of their apartment. But Sal didn't fool Sophia with his fake smile and the cigarette between his lips: he too had been disappointed, and right away he went looking for Vera—from room to room he went, from one apartment to the next, up and down the stairs, calling her name, then smoking on the stoop, then back inside. "Did you find her?" he asked Sophia. "I didn't mean to get her so upset. She gets herself too worked up." He looked for her again, called her name, said he was sorry, and then he heard what sounded like her crying, and he followed this sound and found her in Sophia's bathroom, sitting in the tub, the shower curtain closed. "I didn't mean to get you so upset," he said, "but sometimes you live in a dream world."

And how Sophia hated Sal for being right: they would never see Tony again.

Now Vera stood on a stool, covering her scar as best she could, and Sophia held her arms while Vera dipped her foot into the hot water. "Run some cold water," Vera said. Sophia held her sister with one hand and turned on the water with the other and the bubbles rose higher. Vera lifted her other leg off the stool and lowered it into the water, and then Sophia eased the rest of her sister's body into the tub and shut off the cold water. "The bubbles are too high," said Vera.

Sophia moved the bubbles away from her sister's face and opened the door.

"I thought you would sit here with me," said Vera.

"I don't want to watch you take a bath."

"The water is too high," said Vera. "I'm afraid."

"You're always afraid of something," said Sophia. "What is going to happen?"

"I could slip down under the water," said Vera.

"So I should sit here while you wash yourself?"

"I'm just soaking."

Sophia closed the door and sat on the toilet seat and tried to finish a crossword puzzle.

Vera breathed in the steam from the tub and pushed away the bubbles so that they covered her legs. She could live to be one hundred, she thought. (Steam filled the room and formed shapes in the air and rose to the ceiling and hovered there for her to see.) Her mother almost lived to be one hundred—but no, she, Vera, would not live to be one hundred: the body did what it had to do (it sat in a tub and shriveled and loosened and softened), and when it was finished it did the last things (it failed and pained and stopped and disappeared).

The water grew cold; bubbles popped above her old legs.

"I want to go outside," said Vera as Sophia dried her body.

"Just before you said you were afraid."

"I am afraid." (She could hear the water being sucked down the drain.)

"I'll put your clothes on and you'll change your mind," said Sophia.

"I have to get out of the apartment."

"You can't get your feet into shoes," said Sophia.

"I'm afraid of what will happen." (Water choked down the drain and steam vanished near the ceiling.)

"What will happen?"

"I won't make it back inside," said Vera raising her arms so that Sophia could pull down the red sweater.

"Do you want to be inside or outside?"

"I want to go outside and then I want to come back inside." (The pain squeezed her side and she cursed the cold water as it disappeared down the drain.)

"And then what?"

"I want to do that every day," said Vera as Sophia pulled up her socks.

"And then what?" said Sophia.

They walked down the stairs slowly, both feet on each step, resting after every three or four. They stopped between the first and second floors and Vera placed a pill under her tongue; her mouth tingled; the pill dissolved and the pain in her chest went away. She could do this: she could go down and come back up; she *could* live to be one hundred. "Now my left foot," said Vera with every other step.

The stoop was covered with ice, and the trees, their branches long and bare, cast shadows on the snow-covered ground. Sophia walked down the stoop first and Vera followed, holding her sister's coat.

The wind pressed against Vera's back. "My legs are too heavy," she said.

"What are you afraid of?" said Sophia. "What is going to happen?"

"So many tests for nothing." The ice stretched in front of her and the wind shook the trees above her. She reached for her sister's hand.

"A walk will be good for you," said Sophia.

"I'm not getting better," said Vera.

"You'll get better."

"My face is cold," said Vera (and now she thought, looking down, that the ice was not a fine place).

The two women walked side by side and they were afraid (but they did not reach for one another).

The body took a step; it took another. The cold grew familiar. Vera knew the pain in her side; she knew the church light in the distance; she knew the shadows on the ice and she looked for her mother in them.

"Look at me," said Vera. "I'm walking." She took baby steps and reached for Sophia's arm and took shallow breaths. "This is okay," said Vera. "I'm okay." But the pain gripped her side and she stopped and when she looked behind her she saw that she was not so far from the stoop. The ice stretched before her and the pain squeezed her side and would not go away. She would never feel better than this.

"I'm dying," said Vera. The darkness was above her and around her and the bright church too far in the distance. There was no such thing as a fine place.

"I know," said Sophia, and then she helped her sister take the next step forward on the icy street.

"Look at me," said Vera for anyone to hear.

Chapter Seventeen

≈

LUCKY

(March, 1997)

Morning

Sal was not paying attention: a cigarette ash fell onto his eggs. He stood over the frying pan and tried to wipe away the ash with his finger, but again he was not careful and the ash slipped off the egg and into the melted butter in the pan. He cursed himself and the pan and the eggs and the small pieces of egg shell that had fallen into the pan. To hell with it, he thought. To hell with everything except the cigarette in my mouth. And so he scraped the dry eggs into a garbage bag and finished his cigarette. This is all I need, he thought (the cigarette small now, the burning ash close to his face). He inhaled very deeply when he smoked. He liked to watch himself in the mirror sometimes when he smoked.

This was what he had always wanted: the apartment quiet, only the radiator hissing out heat.

But it had been nice to have someone sitting in the next room. It had been nice to know, as he fell asleep, that Vera was sitting somewhere knitting a scarf. Maybe she sat in a chair at the foot of the bed. She was somewhere. But it was very hard for her to be quiet, and it made him sad to remember that about her—how nervous she was, how life scared her so much she could not sit still for a moment. It made him sad to think that Vera, at the end of her life, was nervous about a million things. She could not ease herself into life; she could not ease herself into death. Yes—that was what he wanted. He wanted to be a person who eased himself through life and into death. He wanted to recognize when he was in the last moments and shrug his shoulders. And he wanted someone with him as he did this: he wanted someone to witness him shrugging and laughing death away. This was the sorrow he felt for Vera—that she could not do this. Her entire life was a nervous reaction. She could not shrug her shoulders and mean it. And he was not afraid to admit that he missed her. He was not afraid to admit that he felt sorry for her, but he felt sorry—and now he was getting to the truth of things—as one feels sorry for a cat that has died after many years of rubbing against your leg. A very nervous cat who hid under a table when it rained and was afraid of shadows, but who crawled onto your lap when you were sick and slept on the rug at your feet so that you were never alone. You did not want to see this cat die, of course, but perhaps you had come to accept it. What you did not want to see—what made you very sad for the cat—was the way in which it died: it balled itself in a corner and faced the wall for days; it looked at you and then looked away, and you knew that death was already inside it.

Afternoon

The weather man on the news said it was not a good day to be outside. It was not a good day to drive and not a good day to walk. It was a good day, however, if you wanted to fall and crack your hip. This weather man thought he was comical. Sal did not trust anyone he saw on television, and certainly he did not believe the weather report, not with such a smart aleck running the show.

But when he looked out the window he saw white, and more white. This morning, he had seen no signs of this coming.

It was true—no one would be smart to go outside on such a day.

But Vera (he remembered) walked to the store on a day worse than this. She left the ziti baking in the oven: what else could she do with Tony crying in the hallway? But that was Vera—anything to put out a fire. And the way she sat in a chair across from Sal and struggled with her boots: surely she did not think he was the kind of person to walk away from a football game and walk to the store for a baseball card; surely she knew him better than that. But perhaps not, for she pulled on her boots very deliberately and said she was going to turn into a snowman out there. "Send out a rescue team if I don't make it back," she was saying. "Look at me, Sal. I'm going outside with only a housedress under my coat. Look at this." He turned away from the game for a second—he could give her that much—but he would not look worried, not for someone who did not know how to let a fire burn itself out. But he did not like the way everyone stared at him after Vera left the apartment, so he watched her from the window. She made her way slowly to the corner, struggling to lift her legs out of and over the high piles of snow on the sidewalk, and he thought: *Walk in the street where it has been plowed!* And he thought this not because she would not deserve to fall should she continue this way over the high snow, but rather because he did not want to be put on trial should she come back with even a bruise on her toe. He watched her reach the corner and walk out of sight. He stayed at the window, even when he heard the others yelling about the game. He waited until she should have had enough time to reach the store, buy the baseball cards, and make her way back slowly through the snow. There was no one in the street. A salt truck drove down the street where the street had been plowed. Sal passed the time waiting for a large icicle to break and fall from a branch, and finally there she was, lifting her boots very high over the snow. He went into the television room and told the others: "She made it. I watched the whole time from the window. She's the only person on the entire street." And then she came inside, breathing deliberately, and she was very loud banging the snow off her boots at the door. "It's not so bad," she said. "Here Tony. Come get your picture cards," and she waited for him at the door.

But now, years later, sitting alone in his kitchen, he remembered most clearly the look on her face when Tony opened every pack and did not find the one card he needed. Vera looked through the cards, as if she could not believe it true, and then she went into the kitchen to stir the gravy.

$$\equiv$$

Evening

He walked into Sophia's apartment and found her dozing at the kitchen table. She had been playing solitaire. There were cards laid out in front of her and the rest in her hand.

"Hey, are you awake?" said Sal.

"I'm awake," said Sophia. She counted three cards and dropped one on the table. She did not watch what she was doing.

"You were sleeping," said Sal. "Don't tell me you were awake."

"I was resting my eyes."

"Is that what you call it?"

"You kept your mouth shut all day," said Sophia. "Why do you have to open it now?"

"I came up to see if you were still alive."

"You must be disappointed," she said.

"Nothing bothers me."

"Maybe you shouldn't be so happy," she said.

"I sleep very well at night," he said (though he had not been sleeping well: his stomach, he told himself).

"You'll live to be a hundred. There's no doubt in my mind."

"In that case, maybe I should get married again."

"You're a very cold man," she said.

"It was a joke," said Sal. "Hey. Listen. I was only joking."

Sophia counted three cards and turned one over. Sal looked out the window and saw that the sky was still white.

He said, "You don't have a meatball, do you?"

"No."

"Do you have a piece of chicken?"

"No."

"Any leftover macaroni?"

"No. I ate everything for supper."

"What did you make?"

"I had stuffed peppers with a nice meat gravy."

"Anything on the side?"

"A piece of pork," she said, and then shook her head. "Not so good. It was dry."

"Do you have any pork left in the icebox?"

"No. I threw the rest in the garbage. It was much too dry."

"I feel like I've lost ten pounds already," said Sal.

"From what?"

"What do I know about cooking for myself?"

"You didn't lose ten pounds," she said. "Look at your belt. You're still using the same belt hole."

"I never said I lost ten pounds. I said I feel like I lost ten pounds."

"You should have learned to cook when you had the chance."

⎯⎯

Morning

He woke when it was still dark, and he felt like something was inside his stomach trying to punch its way out. He walked to the kitchen and turned on a light. The floor was very cold, and outside was all white, and more white. He opened the refrigerator and looked inside. He crouched very low and looked inside the drawers at the bottom. He opened a jar of pickles and brought it up to his nose, and then he put the jar back and closed the door.

What he decided to eat was not so bad after all: three or four artichoke hearts with some salad dressing on top.

But what heartburn it gave him!

He sat in a soft chair and breathed deeply, trying not to think of the pressure in his stomach and chest. He did not believe in taking pills. A cigarette would do for him much more than a pink stomach pill. It relaxed him to breathe in the smoke and hold the cigarette very close to his face. He closed his eyes and felt the smoke around his face; this was working better than a pill, it was making his body very light—

—and then he woke with the cigarette burning on his lap. Even in such a situation he was calm: he stood slowly and removed the cigarette from his leg and dropped it into an ashtray.

He had always been lucky that way.

Once there was a spot on his chest X-ray and it turned out to be nothing. Another time, they found a blood clot in his neck during a routine physical, and two days later they cut it out.

He had been very lucky, he reminded himself, and there was no end to his luck.

He lit another cigarette, reclined the chair, and closed his eyes.

Chapter Eighteen

LETTER: VERA

(November 15, 1993)

Dear Tony,

I promise to you that this is my last. Unless you have changed your mind and want your grandmother to write.

Last night I had a dream. I had a dream that someone was knocking on my door. Your grandfather would not get up to see. So I take a chance and walk to the door. But then I get a terrible feeling about what is behind the door. I can hear somebody crying in the hallway, but this is not only a crying—it is also a laughing! How this can be true I don't know. This is a dream. What do I know from a dream? So I get scared about the door. Should I open it? Should I go back to bed? Your grandfather—he's out of the dream by now. It's just me and the door and what's behind it.

How can I say this?

I opened the door and there you were. You had blood all over your face and on your hands and your eyes were red, and you were holding out to me your hands. You were asking for me to kiss them. You were reaching out for me. So I close my eyes and scream, and I scream some more, and then Sal is slapping me across my face.

But let me tell you. I was not in bed. I was standing at the open door.

This worries me—that it was a nightmare and not a regular dream. I have a friend, a lady who lives alone down the street from here. The reason she lives alone is that her husband is dead. Her two children are also dead. This lady is not so old. She said to me that the night before her husband died and also the night before each of her children died, she had a nightmare. And every time it was one of them knocking at her door.

Maybe you believe this and maybe you don't. But I don't want to take a chance. So I am asking for you to tell me that you are alive and okay. This is just your grandmother being silly.

Also, I wonder about the few dollars I sent to you so long ago.

Please, if you could put me at ease.

Love to my boy,
Your grandmother

Chapter Nineteen

THE REST OF HIS LIFE

(January, 1998)

Tony could hear the coughing of the man in the room next to his. Snow covered the cars in the parking lot. Heat rattled out of the baseboard but he could not feel it, and so he waited under a blanket that made him itch. He liked to sleep with the blinds open. The television spread a dull light around the room. He turned up the volume, but still he heard the man coughing in the next room, so he turned off the television and lay in the dark waiting to feel warm. Outside looked cold: snow fell against the window and melted down the glass, and it made him feel warmer to be inside under a blanket. The room was becoming familiar. No longer did he wake in the night and get lost on his way to the bathroom. He knew which drawer held his socks; he knew what time the man in the next room went to bed and what times he was prone to coughing and when he got out of bed and turned on the shower; he knew the faces of the people who worked behind the front desk. He had not been living in this room very long.

Two weeks ago, someone threw a brick through his window. There was a piece of paper attached to the brick and on the paper was written a date. He knew the date. He had been living on the first floor of an old building on Flatbush Avenue. A few days later bullets were shot into the new window. He was not home when it happened, but his neighbors told him what they heard and they showed him the marks on the side of the building where the bullets hit and when he went inside he could see broken glass on the floor. He called the police and asked what he should do. Was anyone after him for any reason? He said that he did not know. Did he owe anyone a lot of money? No, he did not. Was there anyone he could stay with—parents, a girlfriend? He would be okay, he told them.

His landlord replaced the window that night. He was not happy about the situation. He said that if anything happened to this window he would ask Tony to leave.

Tony tried to stay there the next night, but he could not sleep. His heart raced whenever he heard a car pull to the curb. He kept a light on and moved to the floor. He heard a noise outside, near the door, and he crawled to the window. Someone was playing with the doorknob. He stayed on the floor and could not make himself raise his head. He did not want to look out the window to see who was there. There was no one he wanted to call. He waited near the window, and after a while the noise stopped. He waited a few minutes and then he looked out the window.

He kept the brick and the paper that was attached to it. He put them on top of the television and did not show them to anyone. And when he left his apartment and came to this room, he brought—in addition to his clothes, a bar of soap, a razor, and a hairbrush—the brick, which he kept on the dresser, and the piece of paper, which he kept separately in the bottom drawer.

≈

But he had to return to his apartment to get more clothes, and when he did he found that someone had been there. The lock on the door was broken. A drinking glass sat on his bed. The refrigerator was open and a jar of tomato sauce had been left on the floor. The bathroom light was on. He did not want to die. He did not want to be injured or kidnapped or even frightened should someone jump out from behind the shower curtain, so he backed out of the bathroom and backed through the one room that was his apartment. He stood by the door and waited for something to move. And as he stood there he thought of the brick, which had been painted black. He thought, standing near the door, that this brick had been painted black for a reason. He thought of the date written on the paper. The paper was in the bottom dresser drawer in the room he now lived in. And why had he put the paper where no one was likely to find it? It was a special piece of paper to be alone in the bottom drawer, and he knew exactly the date written on it, and of course he did not want anyone to see it or to know that he separated it from the brick and kept it separate from anything else he kept in his room.

He stood at the door thinking that he did not want to die. It would be okay to be injured or kidnapped or scared by someone jumping out of the closet. It would be okay to have someone jump out and hit his head with a pipe. It would be fine if someone punched him or broke some of his bones or humiliated him. It would be okay if someone raped him. It would not be the end of the world, he thought, if someone—the person who maybe painted the brick black and wrote the date on the piece of paper and attached the two and sent them flying through the window and onto the floor of this room—beat him within an inch of his life. It would not be the end of the world if this person cut off his legs. It would be perfectly okay if this person—who, considering the date written on the piece of paper, was maybe angry at Tony—cut off Tony's fingers one at a time. All of this would be okay, thought Tony, as long as none of it brought him to that point closer than the closest he could come, safely, to death.

But what he was thinking, standing near the door, was that he was not safe—the door's lock was broken, and someone could get him as easily from outside as from inside.

But what he was really thinking about was the date written on the piece of paper. He could keep the paper in the bottom drawer. He could make sure it did not touch anything else he kept in the room in which he was now sleeping. He could do his best to make sure no one looked at the paper and the date written on it. He could burn the paper. But it was too late, really, to do anything about the fact that he had seen the paper and that someone had taken the time to write the date on it and throw the paper, attached to a black brick, through the window of the room in which he had been living. There was nothing he could do about that information. Someone knew him. Someone was angry, someone who knew that date very well.

He removed socks from his sock drawer and shoved them into a large garbage bag. He kept his eyes on the closet door. I do not want to die, he thought. I do not want someone to jump out of the closet or charge from the bathroom or open the broken-locked door and cut open my throat.

⎯⎯⎯⎯⎯

But no one cut open his throat or stuck a knife under his ribs or shot him in the head or back. And though it would have been okay, no one injured him or scared loose his bowels or beat him to within a second of death. He made it to the street; he made it to the subway and to the room in which he was now staying; he made it through a shower; he made it through the putting on of his deodorant and the brushing of his hair and the getting on of his clothes; he made it to the street and into the subway station and finally to the city. He talked to no one; he did not stop for a newspaper. Often, he looked behind himself.

There was getting through work, however—eight hours with people walking in and out the store. And it was his job to stand at the front of the store with people pushing the revolving door behind him. It was his job to watch people—their eyes, their hands, how far they leaned over counters. It was his duty to stop people from walking out of the store with goods for which they had not paid. This was a store with expensive goods. He had been working in this store for a short time and he had learned a few tricks, but he had not yet stopped a shoplifter. He carried a pair of handcuffs attached to his belt loop, and he used a radio to talk to other security guards (they called themselves loss prevention officers), and he heard what the other guards said through a small plastic device which he kept in his ear and which was attached to the radio by a thin plastic wire.

Such was his job—acting like a police officer.

But he was more concerned with who was entering the store behind him. He was vulnerable with his back to the door. It would be easy for someone to get him from behind. He was thinking, specifically, of the person who had painted the brick black and tossed it through his window.

＝

How could he feel safe with someone leaving notes for him at the front desk?

Yes—someone was leaving envelopes with Tony's name and room number typed on the outside. Was that supposed to make him feel safe?

There were two envelopes—one left on the counter that morning and the other a few hours before Tony walked past the front desk on his way to the stairs that led to his room. And was he expected now to continue on his way to his room, the number of which had been typed on the outside of both envelopes?

How could no one see a face?

The envelopes had been placed on the counter, he was told.

"Could you make an effort to see who brings the next one?" said Tony. "It's very important."

He walked slowly up the stairs. He unlocked his room and pushed open the door. He ran into the bathroom and parted the shower curtain. The toilet seat was down, where he had left it. His clothes were in the same place on the bed. The closet door was open; he looked inside and saw that no one was there.

But what he had wanted to tell the man sitting behind the front desk, he thought (sitting on the bed and tearing open the first envelope): Something terrible happened. It happened years ago. It was not so many years ago.

And what he wanted to be on the paper inside the first envelope was not there. He wanted an explanation. He wanted a clue. But typed on the paper was a date—the same one that had been written on the paper attached to the black brick. He didn't need an explanation?

He opened the second envelope.

≈

Tony Santangelo was twenty-eight years old and afraid to sleep in the dark. Each night he jammed a chair under the doorknob. He had not been to his apartment in a week.

On the subway, he stood with his back against the doors.

The reason for this: typed on the paper inside the second envelope was the address of the store where he worked. He was starting to think that maybe this was a job he should not have. He was thinking that the person who had thrown the brick through his window was not happy that he was working in this store.

≈

He was paid to stop people from stealing wallets and belts and handbags. He was to prevent the theft of watches and scarves and bottles of perfume.

Such was his life forty hours every week.

And his life was sitting in a motel room with a black brick on the dresser. His life was going to his apartment to see if the lock had been fixed. His life was a piece of paper in his bottom drawer and two in his back pocket.

Work was no great joy in his life. He stood all day near the front door, sweating in the suit he was asked to wear. He stared very hard and long at customers handling lizard belts. He clicked signals from his radio to the radios of security guards standing on floors above him.

One day he saw a young black woman place a handbag under her shirt, and he saw this woman walk toward the revolving door, and when she placed her hand on the door he told her to stop. She did not stop. Already she was inside the door, trying to push her way to the street. She was a small woman and her face was very dark. He held the door with the woman caught inside. Another guard came to help him, and together they pulled her back into the store. They took her to the security office where she cried and promised never again to steal a handbag from this store or any other store. She cried and she would not stop. She threatened to kill herself. The security manager told Tony to place a handcuff around one of her wrists, and then he was told to lock the other handcuff around the leg of the desk. Someone took her picture, and when it was developed Tony was told to write the item and price on the back. He wrote: TAN CALFSKIN HANDBAG, $175. The police came to arrest the woman, but before they could leave Tony had to unlock the handcuffs—one around her wrist, one around the leg of the desk. He did so and was congratulated for a nice collar. It was his case. When you caught someone stealing, it became your case. You had to fill out a report. It was an honor to do this. It was an honor to fill out paper-work, but you were supposed to complain about it. *God, I have to stay late tonight and fill out some paperwork,* you were supposed to say. You were to say it in a way that made people think it was no big deal to you—this collar, this case. The woman's picture went into a file, and the paperwork also went into the file, and this would always be your case.

Tony went back to his place at the front of the store. People looked at him and asked him what happened. "Did she put up a fight?" someone said. "Did she try to bite you or kick your balls?"

But something else happened at work that day. He was almost certain that he heard someone say his name (his full name), and when he moved closer and listened he heard this person—a young black man with a tattoo on his neck—say the name of the motel in which he, Tony, was staying.

Should he have asked the man about the tattoo?

Excuse me, he might have said, but someone has been leaving envelopes for me at the motel in which I'm staying, and typed on the piece of paper inside each envelope has been a specific date, and this date was also on a piece of paper that was thrown through my window attached to a black brick, and it is this same date which I am now seeing tattooed on your neck.

He stared at this young man as he sampled the cologne.

≈

At night, he did a strange thing.

He listened to the coughing of the man in the next room, and when the coughing stopped he was scared. It became such that he looked forward to hearing this man cough. He sat up in bed and waited. The night passed slowly with snow falling against the window, a noise in the hallway outside his door (someone slapping a boot against the wall? someone banging snow from the bottom of a

173

boot?), the snow turning to rain and back to snow. He felt very alone in this room, even with the light flashing from the television and the faint voices of the people on screen. He wanted to call the man behind the front desk. Please, he wanted to say, could you make an effort to see a face?

Now he was a person afraid of the dark.

It was supposed to go the other way, he thought. You were supposed to start your life afraid and become less so. He was shaking under an itchy blanket. Snow melted down the window and soon it would be morning and he could not go to work like this. He could not stand all day in the front of the store like this. He sat in bed and waited for the man in the next room to cough. He turned up the volume on the television. The snow was falling faster and it was very bright outside.

But here is the strange part:

He fell asleep.

And even stranger—it was a good sleep. He woke up and he was not afraid. Last night, he thought, I was a person who was very afraid. His stretching felt good and his shower was very warm. He stopped on his way to work for coffee and a newspaper.

＝

But the man with the date on his neck was back in the store.

He was smoking and Tony told him to put out his cigarette. He pushed his way through the revolving door and tossed the cigarette on the sidewalk. He came back inside and stood next to Tony at the front of the store. He looked at Tony and smiled.

This is going to be okay, thought Tony. Last night I was one way and now I am another way.

"This is a nice store," the man said.

"It's pretty expensive," said Tony.

"That's okay. I didn't come here to buy anything."

"I don't blame you," said Tony.

And then the man said, "Did you get my messages?"

"Excuse me," said Tony.

"Did you get my messages?"

"I'm not sure what you mean."

"Don't be a fool," said the man.

"I don't know who you are," said Tony.

"Let me tell you who I am," he said, and then he pulled a knife from under his coat. He got behind Tony and wrapped his arm around his neck. He pressed the knife against Tony's throat. Together, they walked slowly to the middle of the store. Some of the sales associates noticed and moved away. The customers close to the revolving door pushed to the street and ran away. "I want everyone to listen," this man yelled to the people in the store. "If everyone listens to me, then maybe no one will get killed. Okay, this is Tony. I want everyone to meet Tony. Say hello to everyone," he said to Tony.

"Hello," said Tony very quietly.

"You need to say it better than that."

"Hello," said Tony, louder.

"Now Tony has something he wants to say to everyone, so I want you all to listen very carefully so that no one gets killed." He said into Tony's ear, "Now you're going to say what I tell you to say. If you fuck up—." He pressed the knife harder into Tony's neck.

"Tell them you eat breakfast every morning."

"I eat breakfast every morning," said Tony.

"Tell them what you ate this morning."

"I had a cup of coffee."

"Tell them it tasted very good."

"It tasted very good."

"It made you feel very good."

"It made me feel very good," said Tony.

"Tell them you eat dinner every night."

"I eat dinner every night."

"Tell them what you had last night."

"I had a sandwich last night."

"And what was on the sandwich?"

"It was ham and swiss."

"Tell them how good it was."

"It was very good," said Tony.

"Tell them you have a family."

"I have a family."

"Tell them you love your family and you can see them every day if you want."

"I love my family and I can see them every day if I want."

"Tell them you can pick your nose."

"I can pick my nose," said Tony.

"It feels good to pick your nose."

"It feels good to pick my nose."

"You wipe it on the side of your bed and that feels good."

"I wipe it on the side of the bed and it feels good."

"Tell them you beat off."

"I beat off," said Tony.

"Tell them how much you beat off."

"I beat off a lot."

"And it feels good when you beat off."

"It feels good when I beat off."

"You can beat off every day if you want."

"I can beat off every day if I want," said Tony.

"You can drink prune juice every day if you want."

"I can drink prune juice every day if I want."

"You can stub your toe."

"I can stub my toe."

"You can take a nice shit."

"I can take a nice shit."

"It feels good to drink prune juice and stub your toe and take a nice long shit."

"It feels good to drink prune juice and stub my toe and take a nice long shit."

"Tell them you're sorry," he said.

"I'm sorry," said Tony.

"Say it again."

"I'm sorry."

"Say you're very sorry."

"I'm very sorry," said Tony, and surely someone must have called the police.

"Now tell them what you're sorry for."

"I don't know what to say," said Tony.

"Tell them you're very very sorry."

"I'm very very sorry," said Tony.

"You're so fucking sorry."

"I'm so fucking sorry."

"You're sorry that a bunch of racist wops."

"I'm sorry that a bunch of racist wops," said Tony.

"You're sorry they killed an innocent boy."

"I'm sorry they killed an innocent boy."

"You're sorry *you* killed an innocent black boy."

"I'm sorry they killed—"

"*You* killed."

"I'm sorry I killed—"

"An innocent black boy."

"An innocent black boy," said Tony.

"You're sorry you killed him with bats and pipes."

"I'm sorry we killed him with bats and pipes."

"You're very sorry you smashed his head."

"I'm very sorry we smashed his head."

"*You* smashed his head."

"I smashed his head," said Tony.

"You're sorry you made his mother cry."

"I'm sorry I made his mother cry."

"You're sorry you made her bury her son."

"I'm sorry I made her bury her son."

"You're very sorry for that."

"I'm very sorry for that," said Tony.

"You're so fucking sorry."

"I'm so fucking sorry."

"Now get on your knees and ask them to forgive you."

"Please forgive me," said Tony on his knees.

"Now tell them you killed him because he was a nigger."

"I killed him because he was a nigger."

"Tell them he was just a nigger."

"He was just a nigger," said Tony, and he could see that people were not moving. He could see that no one was going to move.

"Tell them you would kill this nigger standing behind you if you had the chance."

"I would kill this nigger behind me if I had the chance," said Tony.

"Tell them you would break my head just like you broke my brother's head."

"I would break his head just like I broke his brother's head."

"Tell them the only good nigger is a dead nigger."

"The only good nigger is a dead nigger," said Tony, and it was not his voice. It was not his neck so close to this knife.

"Now tell them you killed my brother."

"I killed his brother," said Tony.

"You broke my brother's head because he was just a nigger and we all know the only good nigger is a dead one."

"I broke his brother's head because he was just a nigger and the only good nigger is a dead one."

"Tell them you went to trial for killing my brother."

"I went to trial for killing his brother."

"Tell them you hired a good lawyer."

"I hired a good lawyer," said Tony.

"You hired a good white lawyer."

"I hired a good white lawyer."

"He was nice and white."

"He was nice and white," said Tony, the knife pressing harder into his neck. Did this man know how hard he was pressing the knife into his neck?

"Everything white is nice."

"Everything white is nice."

"Tell them you went to jail for killing my brother."

"I went to jail for killing his brother."

"You went to jail for making my brother bleed to death."

"I went to jail for making his brother bleed to death."

"Tell them how long you were in prison."

"I was in prison five years," said Tony, who hated this man

behind him. He wanted to live. He was scared that he would die and that he would not have a chance to hate this man.

"Tell them that was not enough time."

"That was not enough time," said Tony.

"Tell them you're a very stupid man."

"I'm a very stupid man," said Tony.

"But you were smart enough to save your life."

"I was smart enough to save my life."

"You saved your life by telling the truth."

"I saved my life by telling the truth."

"Tell them I'm going to take the knife away from your neck."

"He's going to take the knife away from my neck."

"Tell them I'm not going to kill you."

"He's not going to kill me," said Tony.

"Tell them I should kill you."

"He should kill me."

"Tell them I should put a hole in your neck."

"He should put a hole in my neck."

"You want me to cut a hole in your neck."

"I want him to cut a hole in my neck," said Tony.

"Tell them I want to be arrested for this."

"He wants to be arrested for this."

"I want everyone to know about this."

"He wants everyone to know about this."

"I'm going to drop the knife."

"He's going to drop the knife."

"When I drop the knife, you're going to put handcuffs on me."

"When he drops the knife, I'm going to put handcuffs on him."

"We're going to wait for the police together."

"We're going to wait for the police together," said Tony.

"Tell them you're going to watch the news tonight."

"I'm going to watch the news tonight."

"And you're going to be very proud."

"I'm going to be very proud," said Tony.

He dropped the knife and turned around. Tony put the handcuffs around his wrists. The other security guards came down to the first floor and stood near them. Together, they walked to the back room.

Tony was looking at the date tattooed into this man's neck. He unlocked one handcuff and removed it from the man's wrist; he put it around the leg of the desk. He tried to take the man's picture. The camera was not working. The police would be there soon, and there was so much paperwork, and this would always be his case. He loaded the camera with film and took the man's picture. The desk was bolted to the floor. The picture did not develop. Tony took another. He wanted to say something to this man. He was going to speak. He was trying to convince himself to say something.

The terrible part is over, he wanted to say.

He was angry. The terrible part was over. He had been through enough.

He had been through it and now he was here and the rest of his life—what had happened before this moment—was over.

Tony's neck was bleeding. He went to the bathroom and blotted the cut with a tissue and saw that it might one day become a scar. There was that. He might always have that. But the rest of it was over: for several long minutes he was very close to death, and he had been made to say things he did not want to say, he had been made to embarrass himself in front of the people with whom he worked. For much too long he was close to death, and he did a fine job with it—he did not cry, nor did he beg for his life, nor did he lose control of his bowels. But he was made to say things, and now what was he to do about that?

Tony pressed a tissue against the cut and went back into the office. The man was talking again. He said, "This guy killed my brother. I want everyone to know about it. I want news cameras here. I want the *New York Times*. I want Larry fucking King." Someone told him to shut up. "Do you know who you have working here?" he said. "Do you know you have a killer working here?" Someone kneeled on the floor next to this man and got very close to his face and told him to keep his mouth shut.

But with a knife against his throat Tony had admitted things, and what would people say to him when he returned to his post near the store's front entrance?

The police came and put a second set of handcuffs around the man's wrists. The security manager told them what happened. They said they wanted Tony to come to the station later that day to answer some questions. But Tony was not feeling well. He almost fainted as the officers led the man out of the office and out to the street.

"You look okay," said the security manager. "That cut on your neck doesn't look so bad."

"It's over," said Tony.

"You're going to be okay."

"I would like to go home now," said Tony. "Is it possible for me to go home?"

"You should try to fill out the paperwork," said the manager. "Your neck looks like it's going to be okay."

"It's going to leave a scar."

"That's not so bad," said the manager. "Now you can always

182

remember this day. You can look at the scar and remember how lucky you are."

"I can start the paperwork now, and maybe when I'm finished I can go home."

"After you finish, you should go to the station and give your statement," said the manager. "Listen, you're very lucky."

"I don't remember what I said."

"You had a knife to your throat. Don't worry about what you said."

"I feel fine," said Tony. "I'm starting to feel better."

"Of course you're fine. This was a lucky day for you."

"I really think I'm starting to feel better."

"You should go out tonight and have a drink."

"I thought for a second that I was going to pass out, but now my legs are steady."

"Do you have a girl?" said the manager. "Take your girl out for a drink. Spend some money. How often do you have a day like this?"

"I should get started on the paperwork," said Tony.

"Take your time," the manager said. He touched Tony's shoulder and left the office. Tony sat there for a moment—the paper in front of him, the man's picture on the desk in front of him—before he started to write.

Chapter Twenty

A VERY LONG NIGHT

(January, 1998)

Sophia wanted to run away from her body—its wants, its pains, its failures—but she had been up three times already to empty her bladder and she had watched the clock inch forward two hours. She was no match for her body: she fed it and cleaned it and rubbed it with mineral ice, but still it was not satisfied: her swollen hand stiffened, her crooked back ached, her pacemaker grew one minute older. And what difference would morning make?

She boiled water for tea; she played solitaire at the kitchen table; she could hear a television in the apartment below. Her knuckles were thick and she would die with her rings on. The flame hissed under the kettle. She was having trouble with the cards—sometimes she flipped two or three at a time—but at some point she had stopped keeping track, and the game became what it was meant to be: a passing of time: the shuffling another sound by which she could move into the next hour.

The tea steeped and steam rose to her face. She felt a pain in her knee and she rubbed it until it went away, but eventually it came back and this time she let it have its way with her. (Years ago, she saw a man sitting on a park bench, and birds—six or eight or ten of them—were pecking at his shoulder and neck, and the man sat there with a newspaper on his lap and let them have their way, and that was how she felt now.)

She had seen death once—Vera clutching the sheets and sweating her way through it, and at the very end she sat up, confused.

But Vera's body had been failing her for years. She, Sophia, was different: she could live to be one hundred. And she was going to prove it by going for a walk—forget about the weather, forget how late it was!

She changed into a pair of pants and a wool sweater. Rubber bands held up her nylons. She put on her coat and took her cane from the side of the bed and stood by the door. She imagined the stairs on the other side of the door; she imagined herself struggling down, then resting, rubbing her legs, then the next step and the next.

But then she closed her eyes and stood by the door and waited for her body to move. She dreamed what was not a dream—that the ice on the street had turned to slush; that it was raining and the streets were dark.

But there was more to this dream (how easily she dreamed standing up lately).

A car stopped at a light and the kids inside the car watched her and a boy rolled down the window and said something fresh. But she was not afraid: she gripped her cane and squeezed her eyes shut and the driver honked the horn. She gritted her teeth and brought the cane above her head and slammed it against the sidewalk. She watched herself very closely as she brought the cane up and swung it down.

And then the car was gone. She opened her eyes: she was still inside, behind the door, and the person in the apartment below was banging on the ceiling for her to hear.

She changed back into her nightgown and promised herself she would go out tomorrow. The tea was cold. She got into bed and left a light on.

She was trying to think of a way to pass the time when she heard the man downstairs banging on his ceiling again. She picked up her cane, but before she smacked it against the floor she heard another sound—not on the ceiling below, but at her door: a series of knocks. She sat up in bed and waited to see if the person would go away, but there came three more knocks, louder. She walked quietly to the door and looked through the eyehole. A man stood in the hallway— a tall, thin man with short dark hair. His clothes were wet.

"My door is locked," she said.

"Hello," the man said. "Is someone there?"

"My door is locked!"

"Calm down," the man said. "I'm not trying to break in."

"Who is it?"

"It's me."

"Who are you?"

"It's me—Tony."

Sophia looked again. She opened the door but left the chain on. "How do I know it's you?" she said.

"Come on," he said. "You know me!"

She saw that it was him and opened the door. He came in and she made sure her chest was covered. "What are you doing here?" she said.

"I need a place to sleep," he said.

"Are you in trouble?"

"No."

"You don't have any friends with you?"

"No, I'm just tired."

"Do you want some tea?" said Sophia.

"I'm too tired."

"Have some tea," said Sophia.

"If you want to make tea, go make it," said Tony.

"How about something to eat?"

"I don't want anything."

Tony sat on the bed while Sophia boiled water. "I almost knocked on the door downstairs," he said.

"You know about your grandparents?"

"Of course I know."

"You weren't at the funerals," said Sophia.

"I didn't find out until after."

"How could you know?" said Sophia, and then she cursed herself for saying such a thing. She tried to think of something else. "Your grandfather," she said. "I thought he would live forever."

"Maybe I will have some tea," said Tony.

"He went in his sleep," said Sophia. "Your grandfather, he was always lucky."

"I like milk in my tea," said Tony.

"He never let on, but he wasn't the same after your grandmother passed. He lost weight. He sat on the stoop. He walked up to the corner and walked back. I thought he would live another twenty years without her, but look how long—less than six months."

"Do you have any milk?" said Tony.

Sophia took the milk from the refrigerator and placed it next to the cup and waited for the water to boil. Rain tapped against the window. Sophia looked down at the street and saw that the ice had melted.

The flame hissed; the kettle screamed.

She brought in the tea and left it on a snack table near the bed. She did not know what to say to someone with such a tired face.

"Ask me how my love life is?" said Sophia.

"How is your love life?"

"Lousy."

Tony laughed on the bed, but it was a tired laugh, his legs hanging off the bed, his body flat against the mattress. She could sit there with her mouth shut for an hour, and still he would say nothing.

Sophia sipped her tea and waited. She would sit in this hard chair and listen to the rain for a full hour; she would wait for him to say the next word. She pushed the snack table closer to the bed so that he could reach his cup. He sighed and put his arms over his face, and she waited and drank her tea.

"Will you stay here long?" said Sophia.

"Just the night."

"We won't have time to talk."

"I have to be somewhere in the morning."

"A job?"

"No."

"You don't have a job?"

"I have a job," said Tony. "I'm taking some time off."

"Are you going away somewhere?"

"No," he said. "I just need to get away from work for a while."

"I ask too many questions," said Sophia. "I have a silly mind."

She brought the cold tea into the kitchen and rinsed the cups in the sink. But why should she not ask him where he has been all this time? Why should she not know what his life has been for almost seven years? And why should she not ask about that night?

It would be morning soon; soon she would be one minute older.

"There are some things I would like to say," said Sophia from the kitchen. "I know you're tired, but would you mind staying up a short while?"

He did not answer, and when she went into the bedroom to ask him again she saw that he was asleep with his hands in his pockets.

Chapter Twenty-one

SUMMER

(August, 1989)

Secchi was having a problem with his sister Gina, and soon it became everyone's problem. She had been snorting cocaine with a group of kids from another neighborhood, and it had been said that one of them—a black kid about sixteen years old—had been bringing drugs into their neighborhood. This kid, it had been said, was kissing Gina for everyone to see, the two of them holding on to each other, very high and happy with themselves.

Gina was very skinny. When she was not high she was angry with everyone.

If you lived on the same street as Secchi, as Tony did, you saw him one night dragging his sister through the street by her hair—she kicking her legs and reaching up her hands to free her hair. Her father stood behind a screen door and then closed the door and waited inside. Secchi pinned his sister to the ground and smacked her face. He held her face between his hands and got very close to her face and said, "You stinking whore! You rotting piece of filth!" At first, she lay there and took his rage and smiled her way through it. But then she tried to kick her way off the ground, and she screamed back at him: "I'm fucking him! I'm going to tell everyone. Ask me how many times I've fucked him on your bed!" And then, if you were listening closely, you heard Secchi smack her and pick her up and throw her on the ground again, and there were many people standing in doorways and some came outside to stand on their stoops, but no one tried to stop Secchi. If you lived on this street, you knew about Gina and her black friend; you knew that Gina had dropped out of school and had stolen money from her parents, and there were rumors of an abortion. If you lived on this street, it was likely you felt sorry for brother rather than for sister. It was easy to look at Secchi and to know why he beat his sister: in this neighborhood, your sister could put drugs into her nose, she could drop out of school and get pregnant, but she could not have a black friend, and certainly she could not be seen kissing him. It was easy to look at Secchi and stay in your doorway; it was not so easy to look at Gina and know why; it was easier to look at her and see her unwashed hair, the run in her stocking.

"You stinking whore!" said Secchi.

"I'll kill you," said Gina under his weight. "I'll have him come here and kill you!"

"You tell that nigger if he comes here again—"

"I'll have him kill you," she said.

But if you were Secchi's friend, as Tony was, you were expected to do whatever was asked of you.

And so when you found your friends at the park, several weeks later, and some of them were holding bats, it was not a time to ask questions. You were expected to accept the bat that was given to you; you were expected to drive where they asked you to drive. These were your friends, and you were considered a coward if you said no, let's take it easy, let's think this one out. You were expected to get into a car and drive to Nino's pizzeria and wait outside, and still you did not know what you were waiting for, but you were certain this was going to turn into something. When someone said *there he is*, when the others ran, you were expected to follow.

———

"This was a case of mistaken identity," your lawyer would say in a courtroom six months later. "This was *not* a racial incident."

"Tony Santangelo did not swing a bat," your lawyer would say.

But that did not matter when the jury came out of that room. None of that mattered when they walked out of that room, with you sitting there in a dark suit, and the others sitting there with heads down, and the boy's family behind you, leaning forward in their seats, waiting.

Chapter Twenty-two

LETTER: VERA

(January 5, 1994)

Dear Tony,

Please. I had another nightmare. This one worse than the other.

There was no blood in this one. No one was reaching out for my face. In this one I came home and walked up the stairs as usual and put my key in the door as usual, but when I opened the door there was someone else living here. I walked from one room to the next. I called out your grandfather's name. There was someone else's couch. There were pictures of people I did not know. So I started to think that something was wrong. I went upstairs to see your Aunt Sophia. I called my sister's name the whole way up. I let myself into her apartment with the key, and when I opened her door I saw that everything was gone. Everything I knew was gone. There was a young man living there and he turned to look at me. He was moving in slowed motion.

But this time there was no screaming. I cried myself awake and told your grandfather all about it. I wanted him to come upstairs with me. But your grandfather, he was never much for sympathy. So I took a chance and went up to see your aunt. My heart as I opened the door! But there she was, my sister, and inside was everything I knew. I made her walk with me from one room to the next. There was her television set. There was her old bed. There was her kitchen table.

Your aunt is a good woman. I said to her can I sleep up here with you the rest of the night, and she said yes. And to make me feel better, look what she did—she waited for me to fall asleep.

I wanted to write to you about this, even though I said my last letter was my last. I wanted you to know about this experience I had. Let me say now that this will be my last, even if there are other dreams. I have been through the worst and here I am.

It is a new year. Did you know that? It is amazing how in a single day one year ends and the next begins.

Love again,
Your grandmother

Chapter Twenty-three

ANSWER

(January, 1998)

But in the morning Tony's plans had changed.

Sophia woke in a chair with Tony awake on the bed next to her. Her neck was stiff and her fingers cold. She fell asleep watching Tony sleep, his hands between his head and the mattress. She watched his chest rise, and it was much better than static on television or a paperback romance. But now he was reading an old newspaper, boots still on his feet, and how long had he been watching her sleep? "You have to be somewhere," she said, and he told her he could stay a while, his plans had changed. "Let me make you eggs," said Sophia, and so she was happy.

Did he want toast with his eggs?

Of course he did, with cream cheese and tomato.

Now she remembered. But how was it possible to forget such a thing? Tomato and cream cheese. It was coming back to her. "You like your tomatoes sliced thin," said Sophia, and she was right. "You want your toast very dark, and you want cream cheese, not so much, on both pieces of toast, with the tomato slices on top of the cream cheese, and some salt and pepper on the tomatoes."

Tony sat at the kitchen table and read the paper. "Make sure the toast is black," said Tony with his back to her.

"That's no good for your stomach."

"That's the way I like my toast."

"It tastes like ash."

"That's the way I always eat it."

"Try it once a little lighter."

"I won't eat it unless it's black," said Tony.

"I'm going to make myself a piece of light toast," said Sophia, and now she would shut her mouth. Why must she say so much when it was not her place? What did it matter if he ate his toast black? Did she want him to eat something he did not enjoy? Would she not fry for him a piece of cardboard if that was what he wanted? "Maybe I'll make my toast a little darker this time," she said, and her neck was so stiff she could not turn her head to the side.

But how could she make him speak? If she could make him speak about anything; if she could make him turn in his seat and read to her a headline; if he would turn and ask for her help with the jumble; if he would turn and look at her back while she cracked his eggs into the buttered pan; if he would stand and walk to the window sill and say, "Is this a new plant?" But it was something that he had watched her sleep in the chair; it was something that he woke early and stayed in bed and made sure not to disturb her sleep. Not once did she hear him turn a page. And how could she forget: it was something that he knocked on her door so late at night!

"That's a new plant I have on the window sill," said Sophia.

He looked up briefly. He turned a page and said, "I've never had a plant."

"It's nice," said Sophia. "You water it once a day, not so much water, and maybe you give it a little sunlight, and when it grows too big you cut off some leaves, or maybe you put it in a bigger pot."

"It sounds like a hassle."

"It's a nice way to pass the time," said Sophia.

"I don't like my eggs cooked too long," said Tony.

Sophia flipped the eggs and added more butter to the pan. They were fine: she turned them just in time. "I'm hoping my plant will make it to the spring," she said. "Then I put it out on the fire escape."

"I used to sit on the fire escape."

"I never let you sit out there. Who let you sit on the fire escape?"

"No one let me. I crawled out the window. No one said anything."

"And what if you fell and cracked your skull?"

"I went out there when I was young and I used to spit into the garden."

"Where did you spit?"

"In the garden. Sometimes I tried to spit on people. I would crawl back inside before they could look up."

"Why would you do such a thing?"

"I liked to see the person's reaction," said Tony. "But I was too scared to stay out there and watch, so I never got to see anything."

"That's no reason. What kind of reason is that?"

"And I just thought of something else," said Tony. "Do you want to hear something else?" (and now this was something, thought Sophia, this was something very different with Tony talking like this, and she would keep her mouth shut and let him talk). "When I was in high school, I spit on my friend's jacket about a hundred times. This is crazy. I'm thinking about it now, and it's crazy. There was no reason for it. We were walking back from the subway station—there were maybe four or five of us—and the whole way I was spitting on the back of his jacket. It was a gray jacket, and for no reason I spit on it once, and he didn't feel it, and it felt good to do something like that and get away with it, you know, and so I spit on his jacket again, and I was trying hard not to laugh, and then a few of my friends saw what I was doing and they couldn't believe it, but this guy—the one whose jacket I was spitting on—he didn't have a clue. It was maybe a ten minute walk, and I didn't stop. This guy's jacket was covered with spit, and inside I was cracking up. I was picturing what my friend's reaction would be when he got home and saw all this spit on the back of his jacket. This guy was older than me. He was bigger than me. And by the time we got to his house, he figured out that something was going on, and he saw us looking at his back, and then he took off his jacket and saw what I had been doing, and he went nuts. He chased me all over the neighborhood. Every time I saw him after that, he came after me. He was a hothead. He ran after me and cursed me, but he never caught me. It was easy. I ran around a car, any car. How was he going to catch me if I kept running around a car? Sometimes he would chase me for an hour, and then he would give up and walk away, and he would swear that he was going to kill me. I got such a kick out of teasing this guy. I knew he would never catch me. And so what if he did—what was he going to do?"

"What kind of a story was that?" said Sophia. (She wanted him to say more: it did not matter what he said; it did not matter what he revealed.)

"It's crazy to think that I did that," he said.

"One time, when you were very small, you took a knife out of my kitchen drawer and you scratched my walls." She plated the eggs and added salt and pepper.

"I don't remember that."

"You don't remember?" said Sophia, bringing his plate to the table. "I smacked you right in the face."

"You never hit me."

"Not so hard," said Sophia, and then she spread cream cheese on his toast and made sure the tomato was sliced very thin.

When he finished the eggs, his toast was waiting for him on the table.

But this time he did not disappear.

He took her to the beauty parlor, and she did not have to ask. The arthritis was in her legs now, and she was walking with a cane, and Tony had noticed this the last time he was there. He called her and said, "Aunt Sophia, how are your legs?" and she answered, "Lousy. Just like my love life."

What was she doing that day?

Well, she would watch her morning programs, and then she might have leftover eggplant for lunch, and maybe she would cancel her beauty parlor appointment. The streets were icy and what a wind she could hear against the windows. And her cane was no good—she lost the rubber tip at the bottom. "You have no grip with a cane like that," she told Tony. "You put the cane against the ground and it does nothing for you. It slides along the ice and then maybe you're on the ground with a broken hip." But then he said, "Don't cancel anything. I'll take you to the beauty parlor." That was something—he offered without her asking.

She put on a new lipstick; she rubbed her legs with mineral ice; she sewed shut a hole in the top of her hat, and then she soaked her stiff hands in warm water.

What a jump when she heard the downstairs bell!

Imagine that—she had fallen asleep again in a chair.

She buzzed Tony inside, and then stood by the door listening to his shoes on the stairs. But look at him without a hat on his head. Did he want to wear one of her hats? He did not like to mess his hair. Young people did not wear hats, he told her. But she could not leave it alone: she looked through her closet and found an old hat. It was purple and it had sparkles on it and a pompon at the top. She brought him the hat and he looked at it and said, "Aunt Sophia, what the hell is this?" and they had a nice laugh.

He stood in front of her on their way down the stairs. He walked very slowly, and she told him to go ahead, wait at the bottom, she would be fine, but he said no, he would stand in front of her, and she thought: *that's the kind of boy he is.*

But how she worried about his head as they walked along the street.

He held her arm and not once did he rush her, and anyone who saw them would know what kind of boy he was. He steered her around icy patches; he held her so tightly as they walked over snow mounds that she was sure she was floating. She moved her legs and they touched nothing. She could close her eyes and not worry about losing her way.

And what did they say to one another?

"Watch out for the ice," said Tony. "You can't see it."

"You could break your hip on a day like this."

"Here's another patch."

"Hold on. Wait a second. I don't see it."

"Take your time," he said.

"Hold on. Don't let go. I don't feel anything under my feet."

"We're almost through it. Let me bring you through it."

"My old legs feel very young," said Sophia. "You're doing all the work."

But she did not like to watch the wind blowing his hair. She should have made him wear the hat. Who was going to say something about a hat with a pompon on a day like this? She looked at his red ears and tried to walk faster. She was getting tired and her legs were very old again.

"My eggs are old again," said Sophia, and what a look he gave her!

"My *legs* are old again," she said. "I was thinking about eggs."

"You were daydreaming."

"I was standing in front of the stove, and I was making eggs for you. That was my dream. I had a dream right now as we were walking. Maybe I was trying too hard to make myself warm."

"We're almost there," said Tony.

She saw that his nose was red; she pushed her legs forward.

The beauty parlor was crowded, and she did not ask him to come inside. He would come back for her in an hour.

"My grandson walked me here," she said to the woman setting her hair, but then she remembered—he was not her grandson. (She did not correct herself. Why should she open her mouth and correct herself?)

When he picked her up later, he said that her hair looked very nice and that maybe now her love life would not be so lousy, and they had a good laugh.

"This is Tony," said Sophia, and everyone looked at him and nodded their heads.

She heard someone say *handsome* as they walked together onto the street.

⸻

Two days later the sun was out and people carried jackets over their arms.

She sat on the stoop and waved to school children. An upstairs window was open, and she heard her phone ringing. Snow melted on the sidewalk and the water ran into the street and along the curb. Again, the phone. She could hear water running along the street and into the sewer on the corner. The sun on her face was a strange thing. I have skipped ahead in time, she thought. Two days ago it was winter and now it is like spring, and what happened to the time between? All the silly thoughts she had been having (it was the bad weather, she was certain, it was ice hanging from branches, it was an afternoon shadow on her wall, it was the sun falling much too early, it was her always eating supper after dark, it was ice against her window, it was tea getting cold before she could drink it)—such strange thoughts when she watched her programs: that it was not enough to sit in a chair and watch made-up stories; that the people she saw on television were not real, they were tricksters, and how silly to think that she was not alone; that some of the people she saw were dead and some were alive and would be dead and some were alive and would still be so when she was dead, and never in her life had she had such thoughts, not when her husband died in their bed, nor when she dropped a white rose on the box as they lowered it into the ground, nor when Vera sat up in bed and looked confused; but now she remembered the time she felt like this: it was the day she saw Tony's face on the news, and later when she read his name in the papers, what a rush of crazy thoughts when she knew it was *him*, not another Tony Santangelo: there was the thought that she would never be able to sleep, everything was over, everyone she had ever known was dead; there was the thought of her own death, that the room could not be darker, that the lights were dimming and outside was dimming and the air around her face would always be this dark, and these were the thoughts she had been having lately, even with Tony knocking on her door so late, even with his walking her to the beauty parlor, there were these thoughts, and how, she wanted to know, how could she have these thoughts with Tony, finally, after so much time?

It was the television. She had to get rid of her television.

Last night she saw a woman found dead in an abandoned building. She saw a swollen black stomach and a chin chewed by rats. That was what they said on the program: this woman's chin had been chewed by rats. They explained that the body went stiff after only two hours. This woman had been dead a week. There was a fly on her stomach. They explained that this woman drank herself to death. They wore masks as they poked her body and stuck a needle into her side and said that her body temperature was such and such and that she had been dead a week. They wore gloves. They wrapped her in plastic and took her away, and still Sophia did not change the channel. "That's me," one of the men said, pointing to the body.

"That's me right there. That's all of us. That's what happens to us."
How was she supposed to change the station? Were you supposed to
look at your television screen and see a chewed chin and change the
station? You were not supposed to think about these things. It was
silly to think of a dead woman who stayed stiff as men turned her
over. You did not think of such things; you did not talk about such
things; you did not wake in the night and think of the dead woman;
it was not supposed to remind you of something else. How you did
not know the people living below you. How long it would be before
someone broke down your door. You could think of Tony and how
he was now calling you every night, and there was the chance, now,
that he would be the one to find you, but you were not supposed to
think about the other thing; you were not supposed to think about
the boy with a cracked skull, nor of Tony holding a bat, nor of a needle stuck into the boy's side to take his temperature, and this was
the Tony who was calling you every night to see if you were alive,
this was the Tony who would most likely find you when you were
no longer you. And even on a day like this, with the sun on your
bare arms—such an unexpected day—there were these thoughts in
your mind, and you were afraid they would be there until the last
moment, and then what, and you must, you must, you *must* get rid
of your television.

"I called and you didn't answer," she heard someone say, and
when she looked up there he was.

"I was sitting on the stoop," said Sophia.

"I thought maybe you fell asleep in the tub," said Tony sitting
next to her.

"I don't sit in the tub anymore," said Sophia. "I take only a
sponge bath."

ANSWER

They sat on the stoop a while longer. Tony smoked a cigarette. Sophia waved to the school children as they passed.

⁓

"I knew this was coming," said Sophia. "Lately I've been having strange thoughts."

Tony sat in a chair next to the hospital bed. A nurse came into the room to take her temperature. Tony moved out of the way and stood at the foot of the bed.

She could see out the window that it was snowing. *Only one day like spring,* she thought, and then she was afraid that yesterday had been a dream. "Yesterday was nice," she said to Tony. "Wasn't yesterday a nice day on the stoop?"

"It stayed warm enough to melt the snow, and now we have more."

That was what she wanted to hear—she was not cuckoo yet!

Her temperature was fine. The nurse left the room and Tony came back to her side. "What happened?" he said. "You looked fine when I left you."

"How do I know what happened?" said Sophia. "No one knows. Do you think these doctors know what happened? You would think they would know by now. One minute I was making macaroni, the next minute I was on the floor."

"You had a dizzy spell?"

"Who knows what I had? Maybe I had a fainting spell. Maybe you're right."

"How do you feel now?"

"Sometimes not so good," she said.

"You look good," said Tony.

"I look like I'm eighty-two years old," she said. "Look at me. This is what it looks like to be eighty-two years old."

"The doctor said you need more tests."

"They give you all sorts of tests, but they never give you an answer," said Sophia. "Or maybe they give you an answer, and then you go home and take pills and put your feet up, and a week later you're on the floor again and suddenly everyone is looking for a new answer."

"Don't get yourself upset," said Tony.

"This place gives me a headache," she said. "It gives me a back-ache and a neck ache and a foot ache."

"You're a little pepperpot," said Tony, and she thought: *Once, maybe, I was a pepperpot. But today I am an old lady with my ass cold against a hard mattress. This is no pepperpot. You should have seen me dancing with sailors after the war. You should have seen me singing on top of a piano.*

"Are you hungry?" said Tony. "Do you want me to get you something to eat?"

"This food is no good," said Sophia. "They bring you a little cup with pudding. They give you a piece of meatloaf with some brown gravy and maybe some peas on the side. There is no flavor to it. Not even a little salt will they give you. This is not meatloaf. The brown gravy looks just like the pudding. I eat the bread and I make them take the rest away."

"I can get you something," said Tony.

"Maybe if I'm still here tomorrow," said Sophia. "If they keep me here tomorrow, then maybe you'll bring some leftover chicken cutlet from my icebox."

"It's getting dark outside," said Tony. "Maybe I should turn on a light."

"Turn on the light," said Sophia. "I won't sleep tonight. I've been having crazy thoughts. I close my eyes and my mind goes cuckoo. I think about this, I think about that, and then my mind is moving like a train. It goes into one tunnel, it comes out, it goes into another tunnel, it comes out, and then I look at the clock and twenty minutes have passed. This is how my night goes."

"Can I bring you something to read?"

"What do I want to read?"

"Do you want the *TV Guide*?"

"I don't like to read that. The printing is much too small."

"How about a crossword puzzle?"

"That's no good," said Sophia. "I get half the answers and then I get exasperated."

"Do you want me to turn on the television?"

"No, I don't want that."

"You don't want to watch a quiz show?"

"I don't want anymore television," said Sophia. "If you come here tomorrow and the television is on, I want you to turn it off. I want you to take the plug out of the wall."

"Maybe I can just sit here for a while," said Tony.

"That would be nice," said Sophia.

―――――

Being in the hospital was supposed to make you better, she thought. You were supposed to find out what was wrong with you, even if it

207

was the wrong answer; you were supposed to leave with your wrong answer and go home to take pills and soak your feet.

But this was not good. This was something different.

This was two tests one day and then a day of waiting and then more tests the next day; this was sliding under large machines that took pictures of your head; this was wires strapped to your chest; this was needles in your hand and a plastic bracelet around your wrist; this was someone placing a pan under you when it was too late; this was someone turning you while she changed the wet sheet under you; this was walking down a hall with a bag rolling next to you and your gown open in the back; this was brown gravy and cold beets.

This was not getting an answer, even if it was the wrong answer, so that you could go home and give yourself a sponge bath.

Home was the place you kept all your spoons; home was the drawer in which you kept your lipstick; home was the mirror into which you looked each morning (with a picture of your dead husband in the corner); home was the place at the back of the cupboard where you kept the sugar; home was the wooden fork you used to stir macaroni; home was the flat sheet on which you slept and the green and red quilt under which you slept and the blanket you made for someone (but never gave to them) under which you now slept; home was sliding into bed, even though you would not sleep and your fingers were stiff and the corn on your foot was thick; home was sitting in a chair and picking at a bowl of walnuts with the television volume low enough that you could not hear what was said but high enough that you were not alone; home was knowing which button on the phone was seven even though the number had worn away; home was flushing the toilet and knowing that it would make a noise until you jingled the flusher, and it was jingling the flusher and knowing the noise would stop; home was knowing you had to wait two minutes for warm water; home was knowing you had to light the stove with a match; home was hearing the bell ring and pressing the downstairs buzzer and listening to Tony's footsteps on the stairs and looking through the eyehole to make sure and making a place at the kitchen table and giving him a bowl of tubetini with butter.

And what was she going to give him now—cold beets and rice pudding?

"How are you feeling?" said Tony, who brought her a yellow rose.

This is something different, thought Sophia after a week in the hospital.

She did not feel right. She was very weak and she saw her arm move slowly to shoo a fly from her chest. This was going to be something. This was the darkness you saw around your face when it was winter and you were sure it would always be winter.

This was not her home. Whose home was this? Where were her spoons and the matches she used to light the stove? She was not sure about this. She was not sure if the feeling in her chest would go away. Something was wrong. There was an answer. Would someone please tell her the answer? But she was not concerned about her body—only that it would give them an answer so they would send her home. Home was where she smacked Tony for scratching her walls; home was lying awake and seeing the bat in his hands yet never knowing; it was taking it so far, it was taking the bat above his head and bringing it down so far and then feeling a chill and giving it up.

She must not forget that: home was lying in bed with her mind going into dark tunnels, and she would never know.

And here he was, her Tony, walking into the room with another yellow rose. She was going to say something to him. Why should she not say something to him? There were so many questions, and there must be answers, and if she did not ask now she may never ask. There was a time to ask and a time to keep your mouth shut; this was a time to ask, she decided. *Can you tell me just a little bit?* she was going to say. *Can you take me through just a little bit of that night?*

He was here, next to her bed, and what a handsome face above her. She would never love him less than she did now, but she could love him more. What a thought—*she could love him more!*

"Let me ask you something," she said, but he could not hear her. He moved closer and she said, "Tell me something. Tell me about—"

But why should she say something?

This was fine. Silly Sophia! There was nothing she needed to ask. She wanted to know nothing. It was fine with such a face above her, and his hands so quick to shoo away a fly.

Well, there was one thing she wanted to say:

"Ask me how my love life is."

"How is your love life?" said Tony.

"It's not so lousy," she said. "Look how many yellow roses."

Chapter Twenty-four

CLOSING

(February, 1998)

Someone came and bought the bed. No one wanted the mattress, which was stained and torn at one of the corners. A young couple came and looked at glasses and plates. The designs had faded, and so the woman said she did not want them, but the man said they were more valuable that way, and the woman disagreed, and the man said he knew what he was talking about, his secretary's son was an expert in antique dishware, and there was no doubt in his mind that the faded patterns were exactly what they were looking for, and the woman said she still disagreed but that she would let him have the dishes if he wanted them, and the man said he would buy the dishes but he did not want to hear I told you so if he was wrong, since the information came from his secretary, and you know how she is, and the woman said she wanted nothing but the best to come from buying the faded dishes, and he said he detected something in the way she said *faded*, and she assured him it was nothing and that he was the one perhaps having doubts, and at that he paid for the dishes, eight large and eight small. The woman saw a ladle with scratches on the handle and inside the bowl of the ladle, and she paid for it with her own money. She came back the next day to buy two butter knives with letters carved into the handles. Someone bought a candy dish. Someone came and rolled up the rug in the living room and bought that. A man came and bought an empty trunk which he said he would use to store old magazines. He was very happy to find the trunk, which was a kind he had not seen anywhere in a long time and reminded him of pirates and buried treasure, and he left smiling and in a good mood. Someone bought a lampshade and left the rest of the lamp for someone else to buy. Someone bought a clock in the shape of a baseball. Someone bought a bowling trophy for rolling a close-to-perfect game. Someone took old baseball programs. Someone came and looked at the television and played with the back and turned it on and moved the antenna, but did not buy it. Someone noticed something interesting about the light fixtures and wanted to buy those, and he offered to find an electrician to take the fixtures out safely and efficiently, and he came back the next day with a friend and they stood on a ladder and took what they wanted. Someone saw a brass horseshoe on the wall and thought it might bring good luck, and they thought about it for a while and then bought it. Someone bought a desk with a drawer missing. Someone bought a vanity and a jewelry box. Someone bought a small statue of three monkeys—hearing, speaking, seeing no evil. Someone bought the television. Someone bought a lamp without a lampshade. Someone came and looked at the floors. Someone touched the walls and noted where paint was peeling. Someone came and opened the windows. Someone tested the locks on the door. Some-

212

one flushed the toilet and saw that the bowl did not fill, and wrote this information in a small pad. He ran water in the sink and noticed a clump of hairs clogging the drain, and he noted that the water did not go down. He tested the lights and saw that they worked, all except the ones with missing fixtures, and he was happy about this. Someone came and bought the building, which had belonged to the people who lived there, and this person who bought the building divided the third floor apartment, which was now almost empty, in half. Someone was hired to paint the walls and someone else was hired to finish the floors. A young man came while the walls were being painted and asked if he could look around. He said that his family had lived in the building for many years, and could he please take one final look, he was leaving the neighborhood, leaving the city, and he did not know when or if he would come back. And so he walked from one room to the next. Men scraped the walls in the room that had been the bedroom; other men ripped down the ceiling of the room that had been the dining room. This young man looked in the closets (they were empty), then out the window at the street below (it was empty). He was asked by the men working if he would please move out of the way; they did not want him to be injured should a piece of the ceiling fall on his head. Don't touch the walls, they told him. Watch out for loose nails on the floor, they said. He moved out of the way and watched the men paint the walls; he watched the men watch the first coat of paint dry. Outside was turning dark. He asked if anything was left, any furniture or clothing or pictures, or had it all been taken or sold, and then abruptly, as if suddenly resigned upon hearing that yes, it was all gone, everything had been sold, he said thank you and walked out the door. His footsteps were heard on the stairs; the door to the street creaked open; he was heard going down the stoop; and then he was heard no more. The one apartment became two apartments, but the rooms looked bigger with nothing in them. There was furniture; eventually, people. The rent was very high. On one side lived two medical students rarely home, and on the other side a concert pianist who found the rooms quiet and inspiring. The pianist asked many questions about the people who had lived and died there, but his neighbors thought him nosy. He asked too many questions. His music, which he played into the night when he could not sleep, carried into the apartments below.

Chapter Twenty-five

LOOKING DOWN

(March, 1998)

Tony had been driving a while before he realized where he was going. He was going to get on the highway and he was going to drive until he reached a particular spot, and when he reached that spot he was going to turn the car slowly off the road and onto the grass at the side of the highway. This was a raised highway, and he was going to look down to see what he had not seen in almost ten years.

It was winter. People walked through the streets blowing on their hands.

There had been an accident, and there were officers there to make sure he went around the broken cars, and he did not look when he passed. It was Sunday and many stores were closed, but people stood on the street and looked at what was left of the accident. Tony saw a sheet on the ground and there was something under the sheet, and it did not have to be a person under the sheet, and he did not turn his head to look as he drove past the officers and past the flashing red light. It was raining now, and it could have been anything under the sheet. And so he drove through this neighborhood where he now lived, a place for which he felt no sentiment, for it was not the place where he grew up. He did not expect to see anyone he knew since there was no one he knew in this neighborhood. It was Sunday and that reminded him that there was work the next day, but he had decided to quit his job, and that was fine—he had not been happy for a long time, and yes, he knew now where he was going.

Some things he did not want to think about until he reached the highway, and so he forced them out of his mind just as he had forced out the temptation to look at the sheet, to slow the car and figure out the shape beneath the sheet. Inside the car was getting warm. It was nice to be inside where it was warm and to have the glass between you and what was outside. He felt nothing for these streets, nor did he feel anything for the people blowing on their hands, nor did he feel anything for his car, except that right now it kept him warm and separate from everything else, and he could listen to the radio and feel that he was not alone, and so he turned on the radio and played with the dials, but he felt nothing for the radio, nor did he feel anything for the songs he heard, and it was good that he had not turned his head and looked. He stopped under a red light and watched it sway in the wind. He stared at the light and waited for it to turn green, and he forced everything else out of his mind. He cared for nothing except that this light should turn green, and when it turned green he could drive past it and closer to where he was going.

The streets were scattered with holes and it was very rough driving. You had to concentrate and drive over the holes slowly so that you did not ruin a tire, and so that the enjoyment of the ride—the being warm inside and knowing that it was something very different outside—was not disturbed. You had to ignore the drivers behind making noise with their horns, and many of them, thought Tony, were not in a rush to get somewhere, and then he remembered that he was going to the highway and then to a specific spot on the side of the highway, and there were things he did not want to think about until he got there, and so he concentrated on the holes in the street. The holes in the street were a distraction. Everything was distraction—the steering of the car, the playing with radio dials and the listening to music. The driver passing him to the right, very close to the row of parked cars, was a distraction. This driver's middle finger pressed against the glass was a very good distraction, for it was good sometimes to see in other people what you have already learned. It was easy to look at another person, thought Tony, and to know that the waving of his middle finger was wrong, to look and know that it was human to do something like that, and it was very easy to see these human mistakes in others, it was easy to do that and to know you already learned that lesson, but the other thing— the looking at yourself in the middle of some passion or other—was not so easy.

When he was very young, for example, he did not know about those things of which he was supposed to be afraid. What did he know but what he was told? "Watch out for those black boys at the park," his grandmother said as he walked out the door with a basketball under his arm, and that was all he knew. "Don't talk to any dark boys," his grandmother told him, and what did his grandfather say? "Leave him alone. He can handle himself with them." And so it had been said by both of them—there was something at the park of which he should be afraid. It was after dinner. There would be light for a few more hours. There were a few other people at the park, but he played by himself. It was good to have the court to yourself. You could take shots until your arms were sore. You could have a pretend game in your head, and you could play against a boy from school, a boy who was smart and who liked the same girl you liked, and you could pretend your left hand was this boy, you could make it so that every basket you scored with your left hand was for this boy and every basket you scored with your right hand was for you, and you could make believe that if you won—and you always won since your right hand was stronger and more accurate—this girl you liked would take a walk with you and kiss you under a street light, and as you kissed her you would open your eyes and see lightning bugs around your face, and you could catch one in your hand and the two of you could look at it and watch it glow and then get dark again, and it would feel very good to go inside and into your bed knowing that you had kissed this girl and that maybe you would kiss her again, and all of this came from the right hand beating the left, which was the only way it could turn out when you were alone under a basket and both hands were yours.

But you were interrupted by a question: Who came to the park without a basketball? And the answer was that this dark boy watching you play was there without a ball, and he was wearing jeans, and how could someone play ball under such clothes, and then he removed his shirt and you were jealous of his build: the line down the middle of his chest and stomach, which you did not have, which the boy at school had, which the girl you liked would probably want in a boy she kissed at night.

This boy made his shirt into a ball and tucked it into his pocket.

"Do you want to play one-one-one?" he said, and Tony answered that he was not going to stay at the park much longer. "A quick game to seven," said the boy. "Winner take ball."

This was not something Tony had learned. He did not know that winner take ball meant that the person who scored a basket could take the ball and try to score again.

"This isn't my ball," said Tony. "This is my brother's ball."

"I'll spot you two points."

"That's okay," said Tony.

The boy came closer and held out his hands. Tony passed him the ball. The boy took a few practice shots. He was very smooth and he made most of them, and when he missed one he was mad at himself. He was serious about getting the ball perfectly through the hoop and he did not want the ball to touch the rim, but rather to whisper through the net.

Tony was timid on defense. He was not sure how close he was supposed to get, and he did not know what would happen should he touch this boy. It was very hard to play when you did not know the things you were supposed to know, when both arms shooting were not your own, and even if you won you would not kiss the girl from school.

"Come on, now," said the boy. "You can play better defense than that."

Tony moved closer. The boy was sweating, and maybe they would get very close and some of the sweat would rub off on Tony's shirt.

The boy was very smooth and he was serious about the way he dribbled and the way he put the ball through the hoop. It was a quick game, and Tony had managed to score one basket to the boy's seven.

"You're pretty good," said the boy. "You want to play for some money?"

"I have to be home soon," said Tony.

"One dollar a point."

"I don't have any money."

"I'll play you for the ball."

"I'm late already," said Tony.

"I'll spot you three baskets."

"No thanks."

"I'll spot you five."

"I can't," said Tony.

"Then let me use your ball, and I'll bring it back to you here tomorrow night."

"It's not my ball."

"Yes it is," said the boy.

"It's my brother's ball."

"You don't even have a brother," said the boy, and this was something he knew, and Tony thought it would be nice to know things so quickly.

Tony left the park and he looked behind him on the way home. He did not go back to the park for a long time. It was a good park when he was older. You went there with your friends to drink and to touch girls who did not mean so much, and when you finished with the girl your friends were waiting, and you could stay there very late until the police came, and you had learned by that time about the things that should make you afraid, and there were very few in those days.

But this was the kind of distraction you went through when you were driving through streets that meant nothing to you, and you wanted to think about something important, but not the most important thing, which you were saving for when you got to a specific spot on the side of the highway.

The sun was bright in his eyes. The sun was low in the sky, and there were no leaves on the trees to block the bright light. The light disappeared behind a building but a second later it was very bright in his eyes, there was nothing he could do to get away from it. But that was okay. He could see the sign now, telling him to turn right and onto the highway, and it was not very far.

Cars rolled forward and stopped and they moved forward again. It was easy to go into a trance this way, rolling forward and stopping. You could stare at the back of one car for a long time, and you could get to know the details of this car. You could see a bumper sticker that said CHOOSE LIFE and this made you think of something you were saving for later, and so you looked at the hard brown grass at the side of the highway and you saw the many objects lying on the grass—cracked bottles, paper cups, a tennis ball, a folded piece of paper, a coverless paperback, an alarm clock, a pepper shaker, a torn blanket—and you were careful not to slam into the car in front, and then you no longer looked at the side of the road, you were in a light trance, you were in this place and you were in another place, and in the other place you were thinking about the objects you had seen lying on the brown grass and you were giving each one a life, you were tracing the history of each one, but you were not so good at creating a life for an object, you were not very good at tracing each object's path to its present position at the side of the road: you could only imagine a person throwing the object out a car window and you could take it back no further than that. So you thought smaller, you thought of the writing on the bottle's label, you thought of the shards of glass lying next to the bottle, the tears and folds in a paper cup, the teeth marks, the rubber beneath the yellow covering of a tennis ball, the black smudges, the worn frayed yellow covering, the writing on a piece of paper, the lines on a page, the words on the pages of a paperback, the screws and coils and wires that made up an alarm clock, the empty battery case, the individual grains of pepper and the fingerprints on the side of the shaker, you thought of the threads that made the torn blanket, you thought of the hands that worked the cotton threads, you thought of a bed, of a boy in a bed under this blanket, of an older woman standing over the bed and the boy, watching him sleep under a blanket she made with old stiff fingers, and so you were able to create a life from an object, you were able to see the boy curled into himself and very small under the blanket, and this boy was someone you knew and the old woman was someone you knew who once knit a blanket with sore hands, and you were very good at creating a life for this object, but now you were not so good at distracting yourself as the car moved slowly forward on the highway thick with traffic.

But what about the brown grass under the blanket? There was something about the grass. It reminded you of something, and so you thought about this a while until you remembered. This was not something you wanted to remember. The brown grass was a long way from what you were thinking; the brown grass was a long way from a Halloween party with you dressed as a black man; it was a long way from you with black makeup on your face and denim overalls and a pitchfork; it was a long way from the straw hat you wore when you dressed as a black man, and when you were honest with yourself you were able to remember more—that you dressed as a black slave, that you dressed as you imagined a black slave would dress as he picked cotton, that there were no black people at the party and that your friends liked your costume and made comments and it was only then that you realized what you had done, that you had done something you did not intend to do, that you were ignorant and did not think of what you were doing—and it was a long way from the straw hat which looked like the hard brown grass under the torn blanket, it was a long way from the piece of straw you took from the hat and placed in your mouth, the straw you placed between your teeth. The brown grass at the side of the road was a long way from that.

And so he moved closer to the point on the highway at which he would stop.

The car rolled forward. Inside the car was warm. The warm air made him sleepy.

Traffic thinned. He recognized a sign. He moved the car into the right lane and then he slowed down and turned the car off the highway and onto the grass. He waited in the car for a while before he stepped onto the grass. The grass was hard under his shoes.

He walked to the railing and looked down. Below the highway was an empty lot. The lot was dead grass and weeds and scattered garbage. He saw a shovel and a tipped wheelbarrow. He saw several large mounds of dirt. There were plastic bags blowing through the weeds, and he watched one get stuck and he waited for the wind to blow it loose. There was a rusted car missing both doors and all four tires, and on the hood was a stray cat. There was a Dumpster with garbage piled high above it. He heard music, faintly, and he looked and saw that someone had left a small radio in the lot, and it was hard to hear the music with cars passing on the highway behind him. Blowing through the lot were cans and pieces of plastic. He leaned over the railing and looked straight down and saw a tall fence at the back of the lot. There were holes in the fence and sharp spokes at the top.

For a fraction of a second he imagined someone's hands at the top

of the fence. And then he remembered the chase—the rapid slapping of sneakers on concrete. He remembered the feeling that he
had lost control, that something was bearing down on him, that he
was the one being chased.

He leaned over now and felt his stomach drop and leaned farther
and it felt as though someone was squeezing between his legs. In an
instant he saw the whole thing below him. He heard the noise the
fence made when the boy jumped onto it and the noise the bats
made on his bones, and just as quickly it was gone.

The cans made a noise in the grass as they blew one way then the
other. He looked at the cat climbing inside the car. The cat struggled
into the car and made a noise. He looked down and felt that maybe
nothing in this lot would ever leave. The cans would blow one way
then the other, and they would never blow off the lot. No one would
pull out the weeds; no one would empty the garbage from the
Dumpster; no one would come for the car.

The cat came out of the car and waited in the weeds. This was
going to be something. He could feel it. He was breathing deeply
the cold air and bending far over the railing to see the fence, which
was hard to climb, he thought, if you were being chased, and this
was going to be something. He breathed in and felt it in his chest, it
was sitting in his chest, and this was why he had come—it was
building in his chest. The cat stood next to the car. The cat had gray
stripes on its back and a clean white belly. But this was not about the
cat; this was not about the sadness of a cat looking for food; this was
not about the cans and the weeds and the dead brown grass pressed
flat and hard against the dirt. Come on now, he thought. Let it happen. Forget about the cat and the rusty car and everything else and
let it come in with each breath, let it sit in your chest until this
turns into something. Think of the pizza place. Think of the corner

and standing around the corner with a bat in your hand. Think of him running down the street and you behind with the others. Think of him against the fence—the same fence that is now below you— and what he felt when he ran into that fence and could not get over it and was dragged down and into the grass. Think of the others and where they are now. Think of what you felt as you stood there with a bat in your hand and it's the same now leaning over the rail. Think of how you did not swing the bat—you do not remember swinging the bat—and think of the others and how easily they gave you up, and now you were here and you could let it come inside you and build up in your chest.

But you did swing the bat. You stood with the others. You slammed the bat against the ground near the boy's feet. You were too afraid to stop them, but you made yourself a promise and you convinced yourself that this promise was worth something: you were not going to hit the boy; you were going to pretend to hit him; you were going to slam the bat against the ground near his feet.

There was the breathing in now and the building up, and he was waiting for it to come out. He looked down. It was inside him but he could feel it less and it was falling away somewhere but still inside. It was supposed to come out when he breathed. *You made a mistake. The boy moved and your bat came down on his leg. You heard the bone crack. You had made yourself a promise.* But it was lessening inside him, this pressure, this something he could not name, and where would it go? And then he remembered that his friends called him Sambo, his worthless friends called him Little Black Sambo when he wore the denim overalls and straw hat on Halloween, and some of them pulled straws from his hat and put them behind their ears, and what would he say to them now if he saw them, what could he say? Did they make him wear that costume? Did they make him so very stupid to wear such a thing? But they called him Sambo, and when he heard it he knew it was wrong, and now it was coming.

Think of the black makeup on your face and everyone staring.

Think of how you rode the subway carrying a pitchfork.

Let it come, he thought. He had been waiting for this. He opened his mouth. It had to come out of him somehow, this something he could not name.

He leaned over the railing and waited.

ACKNOWLEDGMENTS

The following chapters of this novel have been published in slightly different form:

"Light" and "Ciao Ciao Bambino" (under the title "Light") in *The Massachusetts Review* (Summer 2001):

"Under the Highway," "The Rest of His Life," and "Looking Down" in *Voices in Italian Americana* (Fall 1999).

An essay about the writing of this novel ("Truth in Fiction") appeared in the Fall 2000 issue of *DoubleTake*.

I would like to thank the following people for various forms of support:

my sister, my mother, my father

Jon Pineda

Susan Steinberg

Jay Neugeboren

Doug Arey

Jill Grinberg

Robert Coles

Beau Friedlander

ABOUT THE AUTHOR

Nicholas Montemarano was born in Brooklyn in 1970 and raised in Queens. He holds an MFA from the University of Massachusetts, Amherst. His fiction has ben published widely in magazines such as *DoubleTake, Zoetrope: All-Story, The Gettysburg Review, The Antioch Review,* and *Alaska Quarterly Review,* and has been reprinted in *Scribner's Best of the Fiction Workshops 1999.* He has been a fellow at The MacDowell Colony and a Fiction Scholar at the Bread Loaf Writers' Conference. His first short story collection, *Season of Descent,* is forthcoming from Context Books.